Escape From MH-ZERO

A Northland Adventure

Henry J. Olsen

ISBN: 978-1-944740-00-9

Unbound Adventure Press
P.O. Box 27
Black Earth, WI 53515

http://simplyunbound.com

This one's for John.

Warning (I)

Escape from MH-ZERO is not an ordinary book.

If you read this story straight from cover to cover, you'll quickly become confused. *When did John trip the alarm? How did he teleport into the bathroom? Did he just die and come back to life? What the hell is going on?*

While you're certainly welcome to read the pages in order, your escape from MH-ZERO will proceed more smoothly if you follow the instructions below.

Here's the deal:
Escape from MH-ZERO features branching paths. At the end of each section, John will ask what he should do next and offer a handful of choices. Help John escape by turning to the section of your choice.

Warning (II)

Escape from MH-ZERO is not an ordinary *Northland Adventure*.

These pages will carry you into the depths of John Osborne's consciousness. They will show you a side of John you haven't seen, a side that may surprise you.

Furthermore, some events in this book stray from the canonized storyline of *The Northland Chronicles*. Certain story branches will thrust you into the absurd.

Which paths are real? Which paths are illusion? What actually happened to John in the first hours after he awoke?

In regards to these questions, I will only say that the path that leads to John's escape is both real and accurate. The winning path's events agree with everything you've read and will read about John Osborne and the Desolation. As for the other branches ... let's just say that if you find John getting his groove on, you've probably made a wrong turn.

Escape from MH-ZERO begins on the next page. John is waiting for you.

1

I STIR.

My eyes won't open. Must've been a long sleep.

A crusty layer, stale like the frosting on last year's birthday cake, clings to my eyelids. With effort I pry them open.

Florescent lights hang from to the ceiling. Some flickering, others dead. The air is scentless and slightly dry.

Where I am?

I lift my head. I'm on a table, like an operating table. I'm wearing a white gown.

An IV needle juts from my left arm. It's attached to a long, transparent tube that dangles from the ceiling. The inside of the tube is empty. Dry.

I try to get up. I don't have much luck.

Metal restraints bind my arms and legs.

Good morning, Mr. Osborne. I'm afraid we encountered complications during your operation.

Along the wall ahead are computer monitors and a desk chair. Must be a laboratory. Or a hospital?

The memories rush in like a sandstorm. I was in Egypt with the Marines. It was supposed to be my last mission. Then we were ambushed, and ...

Oh shit.

My eyes dart toward my arm. My left arm. Not right. Left. Left!

Well ... I'll be damned. The arm is there, cuffed to the operating table.

The last thing I remember? Masked men sawing it off.

That means I either got a new arm, or only imagined losing it.

I'm not known for my wild imagination.

I have questions. This table has no answers. Let's figure out how to get the hell outta here. What should I do?

Wait for help.
Turn to Section 3.

Scream like a banshee.
Turn to Section 10.

Try breaking free.
Turn to Section 13.

2

My right arm is tired. My left is still fresh.

I'm not a lefty. My left arm has always been a little weaker than my right. But who knows? Maybe the left cuff isn't as sturdy.

I rotate my left hand so that my wrist faces upward. I then tense my arm and pull.

Surprise, surprise — the metal starts to give.

I grit my teeth and pull harder.

Harder!

The restraining cuff bursts loose from the table like a champagne cork. It clangs onto the floor.

That was easy. Let's try the other side.

I scoop my newly freed fingers under the right cuff and tug at it. Within moments it rips loose. It flies upward and crashes into one of the cylindrical light bulbs above. Glass shards clatter to the floor.

Looks like I became a lefty in my sleep.

Impressive, considering that last I remember I didn't have a left arm.

I yank the IV needle from my forearm. It's the strangest looking IV I've ever seen — a thin white stick, like a tablet stylus. I leave it to dangle from its cord.

I stretch forward to break my ankle restraints. They snap open like a pair of Crown Pilot crackers.

Freedom is mine.

I swing my legs off the table. The floor feels chilly on the soles of my bare feet.

The table I was strapped to is heavy duty. It's supported by a single chrome leg, wider than my thigh, that protrudes from the floor. The table is entirely metal, save for a skimpy layer of synthetic padding on top.

No wonder I have a kink in my neck.

I swipe a finger across the padding's edge. It comes up full of dust.

How long was I lying here?

Tables don't speak. I'll have to ask elsewhere.

There's computer equipment in front of me. All of it appears to be shut down.

Behind me is a metal door. Rows of windows flank it on either side. I can vaguely make out a hallway through the glass.

I have options. What should I do?

Boot up the computer.
Turn to Section 23.

Try the door.
Turn to Section 9.

ヨ

I lie on the table. A Good Samaritan will come to my rescue, no doubt. Right?

Yet as I wait, I can't help but wonder: Why are my arms and legs shackled? Is this the enemy's hospital? Insurgents could come to interrogate me at any moment.

Torture? Waterboarding? Truth serum? No thanks.

Still, I wait.

Minutes? Hours?

No clock. But my stomach thinks it's lunchtime.

Waiting patiently won't fill an empty belly. But hey, you're the boss. What should I do?

Wait longer.
Turn to Section 8.

Try breaking loose.
Turn to Section 13.

4

The computer opened every damn door in this place. Maybe it can do more. Disabling the security systems would be a boon.

I click

Cameras, Sensors, and Automated Defense Systems

A password prompt appears.

Odd. Opening the doors didn't require a password. Why do I need one to access the security systems? Still, I may as well give it a shot. I try the only password I know:

4f5gDser7

I hit enter. Lady Luck smiles upon me. The password box disappears. It's replaced by oodles of security options.

Continue to next page.

As I browse the choices, a slat opens near the keyboard. A tiny metal snake pops out of the hole.

A camera? I give it the evil eye. It zips back into its hole, afraid to stand its ground.

Huh? What's that? A red laser beam aims at my head.

Crap. Maybe I *didn't* get the password right.

I duck, dropping below the keyboard's ledge. Gunfire roars in my ears. The wild bullet clangs into the far wall.

I remain under the ledge. The ringing in my ears gradually subsides.

Silence.

Does the defense system have another bullet waiting for me? Or has the threat passed?

Calmly and confidently stand up.
Turn to Section 33.

Bob and weave towards the exit.
Turn to Section 81.

5

I stride towards the light. The faces become clearer.

My parents. My pals from high school. My buddies from the Marines. More people than I would've expected.

Is everyone dead but me?

Gentle smiles greet me as I step closer. My friends surround me and embrace me in a group hug.

Warmth.

Happiness.

I'm relieved to be free of that creepy hospital.

I don't know where my friends and family will take me, but already I feel you made the right choice.

Thanks for your help.

The End

6

Tap tap tap. My fingers dance idly on the desk.

What to try next? If I'd known I only had three attempts I wouldn't have shat away my first one.

Think. Think. Think.

Got it: "PRESIDENTHERNANDEZ." I key it in.

✳✳✳✳✳✳✳✳✳✳✳✳✳✳✳✳✳✳✳✳

Enter.

`Incorrect password. One attempt(s) remaining.`

Hammersnap. Who am I kidding? This is hopeless. I wanna break something. Vent my frustration.

But I'll defer to you. What's next?

Try a third password out of spite.
Turn to Section 121.

Rip the computer equipment from the wall piece by piece.
Turn to Section 63.

7

Agreed. The scanner seems like a waste of time. Besides, breaking things is fun.

I tear off my gown's right sleeve. I rip the sleeve in two and wrap a piece around either hand. No need to shed my own blood.

I crack my neck. Clench my fists. How strong is the glass? We're about to find out.

I throw a right hook. My knuckles connect with the window.

A sharp pain. A dull thud.

No visible damage.

I reverse my stance, switching to my weak side. My knuckles jet forward. Left fist, meet window.

A resounding crash. A hurricane of glass. Shards scattering across the floor.

My escape route open before me. Only took two punches. Impressive.

A red light flashes overhead. Warning sirens blare. Reminds me of a tornado drill.

I swing through the empty windowpane. On the other side the hallway extends in two directions. The left branch runs for five meters before making a sharp right. The right branch is long and straight, continuing endlessly into the distance.

Which way should I go?

Veer left and follow the bending hallway.
Turn to Section 39.

Dash right down the long corridor.
Turn to Section 74.

8

I wait longer.

No one comes.

The room is so quiet you could hear a rat nibbling on the flesh of a rotting strawberry.

An atonal hum buzzes in my ears. Tinnitus. My reward for years of shooting big guns.

Why am I waiting here again?

Oh, right — because you told me to wait.

I'm having conversations with imaginary friends. If I don't break free soon I'll lose it completely.

My sanity is in your hands. What do I do?

Continue waiting for princess charming
to come rescue me.
Turn to Section 34.

Do something that's actually productive, like
trying to break my bonds.
Turn to Section 13.

9

The door is metal. Looks heavy. Rectangular windows abut it on both sides, offering view of a darkened hallway.

I see my reflection in the glass.

Is that me? I'll be damned.

A tangled mess of hipster hair has engulfed my head. A beard hangs down to my chest.

Rip Van Winkle, my heart goes out to you.

As soon as I find a scissors the hair is gonna go. But first I need to open this door.

No knob. Only a fingerprint scanning panel.

Am I authorized to open it? Does it even work?

I'd bet the answer to at least one of those questions is no.

I can do this the right way or the wrong way.

Sometimes wrong is right. You choose.

Put my hand on the scanner.
Turn to Section 35.

Try to smash a window.
Turn to Section 7.

10

"Help!"

My voice falls flat, dissipating into the dead air. This room must be insulated like an Eskimo's parka.

"Help! Is anyone out there?"

I shout again. And again. And again.

When that doesn't work I resort to yelling cuss words.

Every cuss word I know. Cuss words that would've made Major Dickson blush.

Time for a break. I'm panting like a rabid dog. Probably foaming at the mouth, too.

I've never had to shout for help before. Only seen people do it in movies.

Do you know how idiotic it feels to cry out at the top of your lungs when it's clear no one is listening?

I didn't either until now. Let's try something else. You choose.

Wait quietly.
Turn to Section 3.

Try to break my restraints.
Turn to Section 13.

"Why doesn't every wounded soldier get a true-to-life replacement limb like this one?"

Henry clears his throat and smiles grimly. "That arm is a prototype. It never made it beyond the testing phase. Unfortunately, for reasons that you'll discover soon enough, Pentagon research came to an abrupt halt while you were sleeping down here."

"So there are problems outside?"

"There are, but it's not my place to discuss them with you. You'll see the world for yourself after you escape."

"So I *will* manage to escape."

"Assuming our dear reader doesn't give up before successfully guiding you to safety," Henry says.

"I see." I gotta get out of here. Now.

Ask Henry if he can help me escape.
Turn to Section 77.

12

One more try. This time with feeling.

I rest my hand on the scanner. The electric blue light reads my palm. A message appears:

PLEASE WAIT.

A low hum reverberates from somewhere nearby. The door's mechanism preparing to open?

The humming grows louder, like a high-RPM power tool being pushed to its limit.

Strange. My hair is standing on end. It's almost as though lighting is about to strike ...

Uh-oh.

A thick metal band springs from the panel and clasps my wrist.

A surge of electricity.

Volts.

Pain.

Amps.

Pain.

Legs give way.

Pain!

Body hits floor. Wrist joint snaps.

Pain!

Consciousness departs.

Never returns.

The End

13

Now this is just a hunch ... but judging from the crust over my eyes, the dusty computer displays ahead, and the burnt-out light bulbs above, I'd say no one has checked on me in a long, long time. I need to take matters into my own hands.

I try my right arm first. The restraining cuff is just loose enough for me to rotate my arm. I turn my wrist so that it faces the ceiling, flex ... and pull!

The metal cuff digs into my skin. I pull harder.

Sweat gathers on my brow. Streams of red trickle from my wrist.

Pull.

Pull!

Enough! I let my arm go limp. The cuff hasn't budged.

What should I try next?

Try to wiggle free.
Turn to Section 15.

Try my other arm.
Turn to Section 2.

14

MAIN EXIT

A smooth steel panel. Not a single dent or scuff. No handle. No keyhole. No palm scanner.

Above the door is a small circular hole. A camera?

This facility is deader than an Alaskan fireworks shop in January. I doubt anyone is watching me.

All these defensive measures are automated. And there doesn't seem to be a manual disarm.

What the hell was the security engineer thinking? What kind of idiots built this place?

Hammersnap! I bang on the door.

THUMP!

An enormous sound. My hairs stand on end. My left fist rests in a crater nearly an inch deep.

Hmm ... I didn't expect this.

I try my right fist, throwing it as hard as I can.

Yeouch! Pain surges through my knuckles.

I shake the hand. Nothing broken. But my old friends Black, Blue, and Purple, too, will visit soon.

So ... what's the deal with my left hand? It looks ordinary. Natural.

I run my still-throbbing right fingers down my left arm. It feels like an arm. Even the hairs feel soft and silky smooth.

I slide my hand up the arm to my shoulder.

Hmm?

I tug back the sleeve, exposing my shoulder. A lumpy ring of scar tissue encircles my shoulder joint.

Good morning, Mr. Osborne. I'm afraid we encountered complications during your operation.

I lost my arm in Egypt. Did the doctors graft it back on? Or did they give me a new arm?

Find a doctor and I'll have my answer.

Paging Doctor Limbs-a-lot. An angry patient with a fistful of questions is waiting for you in room three.

Focus, John. Focus.

The arm may be my ticket out of here.

I bash at the door, leaving another fist-sized dent. There's no pain when my hand impacts the steel. Only mild discomfort, like I'm hitting something pliable. Pliable like an Egyptian insurgent's face.

I assault the door. Punch upon punch. Divot upon divot upon divot.

The dents grow wider. Deeper. They merge to form mountains and valleys of steel.

My arm doesn't tire. I could do this all day.

I pause. A voice overhead:

"Please remain calm and wait for the appropriate personnel to come to your assistance. Do not try to escape, or I will have no choice but to respond with lethal force."

A threat. But is there anyone here to enforce it?

No one except the computer. Is the computer itself dangerous?

What should I do?

Keep pounding at a steady, measured clip.
Turn to Section 78.

Stop and wait.
Turn to Section 54.

Try to bust the door open with one well-placed hit.
Turn to Section 26.

15

I try to wriggle free.
Wiggle my hips. Twist my arms. Jiggle my legs.
Shake shake shake.
Shake shake shake.
Shake your ...
No. This isn't going work.

Try my left arm.
Turn to Section 2.

"What's special about my new arm?"

"It's a unique specimen," Henry offers with a smile. "I suppose I can tell you that it's called SPEAR — Strength and Precision Enhanced Arm Replacement. Once you unshackle yourself from that table, which I trust you'll manage soon enough, you'll begin to discover what it's capable of. It offers incredible strength as well as pinpoint accuracy."

"Are you telling me I have a super arm?"

"That is exactly what I'm telling you, John." Henry beams at me proudly.

I'm still not convinced this guy is who he says he is. He does seem to be warming up to me, though. If there's even a hint of truth in what he's telling me, it'd be worth my while to ask more questions.

I already have one in mind.

Ask if there are any precautions I should take when using the arm.
Turn to Section 77.

17

Patience.

I hear the gas seeping in. I'll try to wait it out.

Holding my face up to this hole is uncomfortable. But it's a helluva lot better than breathing the poison behind me.

I wait. And wait. The supply of gas seems endless. And once it stops, then what? Will the poison dissipate? Gradually become inert?

Or will it slowly seep through this hole, right past my mouth and nose?

I try to reposition my face to make the seal tighter. My only reward is more bloody gashes across my cheeks.

Brain getting slower. Hard to stand in this awkward position. Need to take a break.

Just a short break.

I collapse backward onto the floor. The soft, warm air welcomes me like an old friend's embrace.

It's been real, dear reader.

Thanks for sticking with me until

The End

18

I don't want to spend more time on this computer than I have to. I abandon it, not bothering to shut it down.

On my way out, I step past the restraining table. How long was I lying there?

Outside of the room there's a hallway that branches right and left.

The right branch is a seemingly endless corridor. The left branch runs straight for only a few meters before making a sharp turn.

Do I want to take a long stroll or veer into the unknown?

Take the long path right.
Turn to Section 112.

See what lies around the bend to the left.
Turn to Section 83.

19

Are you serious? You won't let me hack off this disease-carrying monstrosity of fuzz?

Do you think I'm some kind of hipster? Or maybe you're worried that the rats living in my beard will bite me while I'm trying to trim. Rabies *is* high on my list of things I'd rather avoid ...

But seriously. You won't reconsider?

Off with my hair!
Turn to Section 51.

I don't need to change a thing. The world will love me as I am.
Turn to Section 97.

20

"I'd like to know what to do first."

Henry quirks an eyebrow. "That's unexpected. You've always struck me as a guy who likes to stay three steps ahead of the opposition. Nevertheless, I shall deliver.

"After you break free of that table — I believe you can manage that much by yourself — be careful about how you use the computer. Only one task is essential to your escape. You must accomplish it and then log off immediately. That should get you started on your way."

I nod. "Alright. Sounds easy enough."

Consider what to ask next.
Turn to Section 77.

21

I extend my arm like a jousting lance and charge across the room.

My fist hits the door. It makes an inconsequential dent. A start but not enough.

I pound more craters into the door. Slowly make progress.

Slowly.

Groggy. Tired.

I sit down. Close my eyes.

Half-awake. Half-asleep.

My folly becomes clear.

The arm's power begins and ends with the arm. Running at the door was a waste. I was using the power of my legs instead of the arm's strength.

Not that it matters, for now I'm at

The End

22

I'm on an elevator platform. It goes up. It likely leads out. These big rigs came from somewhere, after all. Somewhere outside.

I don't know why Dr. Doctor didn't suggest using the elevator to escape. May as well see if it works before relegating myself to a hike down the endless hallway.

I find the control panel near the elevator's edge. The controls are simple. One red lever with two positions: Up and Down. Up goes up. Down goes down.

The lever is in the down position. I must be at the bottom.

Let's give this a try. I push the lever up. Somewhere beneath the platform an engine groans, awakening from a long slumber. The elevator begins a slow ascent up the inclined shaft.

The dead doctor's note mentioned there might be trouble topside. I tighten my grip around the SIG Sauer. I prefer a meatier gun, but the SIG should be ample for self-defense.

As the platform continues to rise, the lights overhead flicker. The flickering is barely noticeable at first, but it soon becomes serious, the brownouts lasting for several seconds.

I didn't anticipate electrical issues. Hopefully everything holds out until —

Suddenly the lights fail.

Pitch black. I'm like a kid trapped in a trash can.

The good news? I'm still moving. The elevator's motor seems unaffected. I'll just have to sit tight and see —

The platform jerks to a halt. I stagger forward. The SIG slips from my hand and clatters to the floor.

Crap.

I fall onto my hands and knees. Gotta find it.

Not here ... not there ... maybe ...

Here we go. I grasp the pistol awkwardly with my left hand. My fingers fumble for the grip.

One of my fingers knocks the trigger with unexpected force.

A blinding flash. An eardrum-bursting boom. An excruciating pain in my chest.

I slump backward. How the hell did I pull the trigger? My left hand barely grazed it ...

I breathe in and out in ragged gasps. Must've punctured a lung. Gonna die here alone in the dark, just like Dr. Doctor.

If someone uncovers my body will they think I was a suicide? Will they think I murdered the doctor before killing myself? Is there anyone left in this world to find my corpse?

I close my eyes. The answers no longer matter. I've got a one-way ticket to

The End

Six flat screen monitors cling to the wall. On a ledge below the monitors sit a keyboard and mouse. There's only a single office chair, suggesting this is a one-man workstation.

Was this computer used to keep tabs on my condition? I squint at the shadowy keyboard. The maintenance crew needs to do something about all the dead light bulbs in this place.

Found it. The computer's power button

I press it. The keys glow blue. A lone monitor above keyboard springs to life. The other five remain blank.

The computer runs some boot-up diagnostics. The usual crap.

Keyboard detected. Hard Disk D corrupt. Ethernet adapter operable. Battery condition critical.

A password screen appears. The cursor blinks, taunting me like a Chinese water torture device.

I take the chair. Crack my fingers.

Challenge accepted. What to type? Let's try "USMARINES" — all caps.

****

I hit enter.

Incorrect password. Two attempt(s) remaining.

Looks like I'm on a short leash. What should I do?

Try again.
Turn to Section 6.

Go look at the door instead.
Turn to Section 9.

I pass through the doorway into an expansive, high-ceilinged room. You could nearly fit a baseball field in here.

Light streams in from semi-transparent skylights in the ceiling. The weather outside looks sunny.

Three canvas-topped FMTVs, suitable for hauling troops or equipment, are parked here. Near the trucks are tables littered with rifles, pistols, grenades, and flak jackets. Metal lockers line the walls. The lockers are probably stuffed with even more weapons and gear.

This looks like an operations room. Troops could've gathered here before setting out on a mission.

Another possibility is that this is the facility's security headquarters. The first line of defense.

There's plenty of stuff to check out. Where should I start?

Take a look at the trucks.
Turn to Section 92.

Dig through the lockers.
Turn to Section 114.

Search for a door.
Turn to Section 61.

Scour the tables of equipment.
Turn to Section 99.

25

4f5gDser7

Enter.

The password prompt disappears. Must've gotten it right.

Zai-jian, Mr. Computer. It's been real.

I stand up and walk away.

A loud bang. A crippling wave of pain.

A bullet in the head.

I'm brain dead.

The End

26

A full-power punch? Sounds risky.

I don't know how this limb works. Maybe I'm already using everything it's got.

But hell, it couldn't hurt to put more oomph into it.

I growl. Wind up. Prepare to launch a megaton punch.

My fist careens forward at warp speed.

Twisting metal. Screeching steel.

When the cacophony subsides I'm up to my elbow in door.

Believe and you can achieve. My kindergarten teacher wasn't making that shit up.

I extract my arm from the ragged hole. The door's steel is over an inch thick.

Over an inch of steel? Christ! This arm packs serious heat. Better yet, I feel no fatigue. A couple more punches like that and I'll be outta here.

Huh?

I cock my head. I hear a hissing sound. The air overhead is shimmering.

Gas streams into the room. Invisible gas.

I'd rather not find out what kind.

Run to the room's far corner.
Turn to Section 44.

Keep hitting the door as hard as I can.
Turn to Section 40.

Hold my breath.
Turn to Section 57.

27

"What's the best way out of this place?" I ask.

Henry chuckles good-naturedly. "That's the million dollar question, isn't it? Well, I suppose there's nothing wrong with giving you a hint. But first you must decide if you want a tip that will help you now or a tip that will help later?"

"I can only choose one?"

"Only one."

Which tip should I take?

Ask about now.
Turn to Section 20.

Ask about later.
Turn to Section 48.

28

Fair enough. Bashing doors tuckers a man out.

I plop myself down on the floor, lean against the battered door, and close my eyes. I'm more tired than I thought.

Sleepier and sleepier.

It doesn't occur to me that gas is leaking through the fresh array of holes in the door and affecting my brain.

Before long I find myself at

The End

Seriously? Shouldn't we search for more important things?

But, well, now that you mention it ... it does seem like I've been out a long time. No harm in making sure Little John is still combat-ready.

I dig through the file system. There has gotta be a stash of hot videos. I'd even settle for a collection of stills.

Grandma Osborne, if you're up there watching me from the great beyond, I suggest you avert your eyes.

Here we go. A folder:

XXX Classified

It contains movie files, ranging in length from five minutes to two hours.

Hmm. I was unconscious in this room for some time. A grease-slathered nerd probably jacked it in this chair while I was shackled to that table, unaware.

Yewwwk.

But what's done is done. Gotta let it go. This clip sounds interesting:

Long John Silver's Hidden Booty

I click. An error box appears.

Cannot open. File may be corrupt. Please check the status of your disk.

Right. One of the hard drives is rotten. Let's try a different video:

Invasion of the Sausage-Licking Zombies

Same problem. Corrupted file. I try a couple more. No luck.

Little John is gonna have to hold tight a little longer.

Look for information about how to escape.
Turn to Section 68.

Ditch the computer and try the door.
Turn to Section 9.

30

Fresh air.

Where?

I scan the room. There's nothing I haven't already seen. I glare at the opposite door. If only it would open ...

Wait. I got it! There's a hole, the one I punched, in the main exit door.

An air hole.

I dive at it mouth-first. The ragged steel edge slices open my cheek. Blood dribbles down my chin and neck.

Only a flesh wound.

I press my face tight into the hole. Take a deep breath.

Fresh air! Disaster averted.

I can only stand here so long. We gotta choose our next move wisely.

Wait for the gas to stop.
Turn to Section 17.

Try to resume beating the door down immediately.
Turn to Section 47.

∃1

"I think you're making the right choice," the man says.

"We'll see. How does this work?"

"Just close your eyes. You'll wake up back where you started."

I shut my eyes. I'm still aware of being in the large room. Still feel my bare feet on the cold floor.

My consciousness begins to hover.

Up.

Away.

"A parting tip." The man's voice is faint. "Be sure to take care of that facial hair. You don't want the people outside to see you with an overgrown beard like that. Not in this world."

"But you said I won't remember anything." My voice feels distant, barely my own.

"You won't. But your guide will. Trust them."

I try to respond.

I have no mouth.

Continue to next page.

An irresistible force sucks me through dark, empty space, tugging me towards a destination unknown.

Soon the darkness breaks. I'm in this room where this all began. I look down at myself from above.

My body rests peacefully on the metal table.

I feel myself being pushed down. Down into my unconscious self.

Mind and body reunite. A haze engulfs my brain.

Black. Pitch black.

Where am I?

Wake up.
Turn to Section 1.

32

I type 4f5gsDer7 and press enter. The password box disappears.

Same password? Then why ask for it twice?

I look for information about this building. What a mess of a file system.

Cat videos

XXX Classified

Write or Die

Solitaire

A cell-phone-sized slat opens near the monitor. A narrow, tube-like object snakes up from the hole.

A camera? It briefly regards me before retreating.

A red beam appears. A translucent line. It aims at my forehead.

Flash. Bang. Screams of pain.

Did I mistype the password? Or did I have the wrong one to begin with?

You'll have to figure this one out. I've already reached

The End

33

I emerge from the safety of the ledge and stand tall.

The red laser has vanished. The computer must think it got me good. What a sucker.

No reason to stay here. I break toward the door at a fast trot. I'm just past the restraining table when the boom erupts.

My head is an explosion of pain. I hit the floor.

Tricked by a computer!

A.I. must've come a long way while I was sleeping.

The End

34

I wait.

Waiting.

Wait. Waaaaaaait.

Wait!

Nothing happens.

Nothing.

Absolutely nothing.

Why would you forsake me to this horrifying fate?

Yeah, that's right. I'm talking to *you.*

Gonna plead the fifth, huh? Fine.

I stare blankly ahead. Angry. Fuming.

I blink.

A man materializes in front of me.

I blink again.

He's still there. He's wearing a black t-shirt and blue jeans. Half-a-week's worth of stubble darkens his jaw.

I close my eyes and shake my head.

When I reopen my eyes the man is still there. He smiles. "Hi there, John."

"Who the hell are you?"

"I'm Henry J. Olsen, author of *The Northland Chronicles.* And you, John Osborne, are my greatest creation."

"What in the devil's name are you talking about?"

"It's actually pretty simple. You see, John, you are a fictional character. Right now you're playing the feature role in my latest book, *Escape from MH-ZERO.*" The man emphatically raises a finger. "*Escape from MH-ZERO* is a gamebook, a book in which the reader chooses the protagonist's path forward. Gamebooks ordinarily provide hours of fun for hero and reader alike. Most readers enjoy *helping* the hero make forward progress. Our current reader, however, intends to do nothing of the sort. This reader has decided that they want you to stay in this room." The man looks to the ceiling, as though addressing the gods above. "This reader is a peculiar reader, indeed."

Reader? *MH-ZERO?* Feature role? Sounds like I'm a pulp-fiction superhero.

What a crock of shit. But maybe this joker will help me get outta here if I play along.

Continue to next page.

"So, you're saying I'm inside a book?"

"That's right, John."

"And this room?"

"Everything. Everything is part of the book," he says. "I must say that you're taking this better than I expected. You're supposed to be quick of both mind and foot, but slow to trust others." He winks at me. "Maybe I don't know you as well as I thought."

What's this guy's deal? His screws aren't just loose; his threads are completely stripped.

But, since it doesn't look like I'll be escaping anytime soon ...

"Mind if I ask you a few questions?" I ask.

"Not at all. You can ask me anything."

Well, what's it gonna be?

Be pragmatic.
Ask: "What's the best way out of this place?"
Turn to Section 27.

Humor this guy's delusions.
Ask: "What inspired you to create me?"
Turn to Section 75.

Feed my curiosity.
Ask: "What's the deal with my arm?"
Turn to Section 89.

35

I place my right hand on the scanning panel.

A line of blue fluorescent light appears along the scanner's top edge. It sweeps top-to-bottom across the panel and disappears.

Red text appears on an LED screen above the scanner:

SCANNING ERROR. PLEASE TRY AGAIN.

A scanning error? Or maybe my hand isn't authorized to open the door?

I see two options.

Try the scanner again.
Turn to Section 12.

Break a window.
Turn to Section 7.

36

I search for more information. I'm soon derailed by an on-screen prompt:

You have been viewing classified documents. Please enter the appropriate password to confirm you identity.

What a hassle.

Do I need more information about this place? I could ditch the computer and escape the old-fashioned way, by trial and error. Another option is to re-enter the password I used to log in.

What do you suggest?

Throw my hands up and walk away.
Turn to Section 41.

Try keying in "4f5gDser7."
Turn to Section 32.

37

Fiddling with individual controls sounds like a waste of time. Why not turn up all the lights?

I drag the main slider as far to the right as it will go. The lights respond without hesitation.

Brighter. Brighter. Too bright! I lift an arm to shield my eyes.

A resounding crack.

A plunge into darkness.

Only the glow of the computer screen remains.

I drag the slider back and forth, trying to revive the lights.

No good. Must've blown a fuse. Where is the circuit breaker?

I click back to the main control panel. Maybe a full system reboot will do the trick.

Let's see here ... Huh?

A warning message appears:

Battery critical. Shutting down now.

The computer commences its shutdown routine. The monitor goes black.

No light. No light anywhere.

Minutes tick by. I wait for my eyes to adjust to the darkness.

Wait. Wait. Wait.

No good. There is literally no light. Not a single photon.

Was the building running on a backup generator? Was that why the lights were so dim?

No more waiting. I should try to find a light.

I abandon the chair and stumble around the room. Searching. Scouring. After a few hours of blind exploring I give up.

One blind mouse. Nowhere to run.
Days pass.
Thirsty. Parched.
Escape is futile. I curl into a ball.
Sleep comes. The long sleep.

The End

38

Patient Status

The file is a spreadsheet. A log with dates and notes. The first entry is from June 15th, 2026 — the day after I lost my arm:

`Operation successful. Condition stable.`

I scroll down the page. Most of the entries are mundane updates about my condition. The document's author thought I'd wake up from my coma within days. Maybe weeks. There are mentions of cutting my hair. Trimming my beard. Changing my nutrition. Trying different drugs.

Weeks pass. Months. The comments become pessimistic.

`Real possibility that brain death has already occurred.`

2026 flips to 2027. Interest in my condition wanes. Weekly updates become monthly. Eventually updates come only on the first of the month.

I keep scrolling.

`No change.`
`No change.`
`No change.`
`No change.`

2028. 2029. 2030.

`No change.`
`No change.`
`No change.`

2031. 2032. 2033.

I reach the bottom.

February 1st, 2033:

`No change. Good luck, Osborne. A`

frightening world awaits you should you ever wake up.

February 1st, 2033. Nearly seven years after I lost my arm.

The news hits me like a shovel to the nose. I've been sleeping for seven years. Maybe more.

How has the world changed? Are my friends and family still alive? Still waiting for me? Did they know I was here?

I need answers. Let's get off this computer and start looking.

Finish up on the computer.
Turn to Section 53.

Look for information about how to escape.
Turn to Section 36.

39

I jog left down the hallway. After rounding the sharp right corner I skid to a halt, nearly crushing my nose on a monolithic sheet of steel.

LOADING BAY - AUTHORIZED PERSONNEL ONLY

It's a blast door. A single panel that opens and closes vertically. Beside it is another fingerprint scanner.

My hand didn't work on the last panel. It's not gonna work here.

The alarm system continues to blare. I wanna get outta here before I go deaf. Let's keep moving.

Turn around and run down the other hallway.
Turn to Section 74.

40

Little boy Johnny punched at the door.

He pounded and hammered 'til the door cried, "No more!"

But for little boy Johnny it was too little, too late.
The invisible poison had sealed his fate.
Johnny sat on the floor and leaned on the steel.
He slipped into a dream. He thought it was real!
"Just a little rest," he said. "I'm on the mend."
No, Johnny, I'm sorry, but this is

The End

41

Computers are more hassle than they're worth.

I stand up and walk away. Before I've taken three steps, I hear a faint whirring, like a fan, buzzing in my ear.

I glance back. A shimmering red beam is pointing at the bridge of my nose.

A flash. A crack.

A painless death.

The End

42

Sounds like a good way to use my head.

There's not much room to work with. I press my body flat against the door opposite the main exit.

Deep breath. Count to three.

I launch from the door and barrel across the short corridor. I lower my head and collide with the main exit door.

Rock beats scissors.

Scissors beats paper.

Steel beats bone.

Bone beats brain?

Where am I? I'm flying through empty space. No floor. No ceiling. Just white, like fluffy clouds.

Scenes from my life surround me.

I see myself scoring my first touchdown. Driving my Ford Mustang around the countryside. Joining the Marines. Embarking on missions all around the globe.

The final scene is of me accepting Colonel Stearns' request to take on one final mission: Egypt.

Continue to next page.

The white haze fades to black. A vague, phosphorescent tunnel swirls before me. A path through the darkness.

Friends and family stand at the tunnel's end. They wave at me.

They want me to join them. I want to see them, too. But a hollow feeling in my gut is telling me that what I want isn't what I need.

What should I do?

Walk towards the light.
Turn to Section 5.

Turn and venture into the darkness.
Turn to Section 59.

43

The buried shall rise.

I spot a red lever, hidden behind a pallet crate. The lever controls the platform. Push up and the elevator goes up. Pull down and … you get the picture.

The lever is in the down position. The platform probably stopped automatically when it reached the bottom. We'll assume it does the same at the top.

I push the lever up. Gears groan beneath my feet. The platform rumbles to life and ascends the angled tracks. Escape is nigh.

What will I find outside? How much time has passed? The answers lie at the top of this elevator shaft. I can —

Huh?

The lights flicker. The flicker was subtle. Was it just my —

The lights go out. They stay off for a second … two seconds. They struggle back to life.

What's going on?

The elevator's motor churns, propelling the platform upward.

The lights cut out again. Two seconds pass.

Six seconds.

Twelve seconds.

I don't think the light is coming back. Fortunately, the elevator continues its ascent. I'll get out of here, darkness be damned.

I reach for the control lever.

Strange. I can't find it. Did I step away from it?

I feel around for the lever, lurching through the darkness. I step forward. My toes find nothing but air. The platform's edge. Best to stay put until I get some light.

Whoah!

The platform jerks to a sudden stop. I stumble forward and slam into a sloped metal wall — or is the floor?

I'm rolling. Faster. Faster.

My hands claw for grip. For a handhold.

I roll faster, faster, faster. My head collides with something hard. My skull cracks.

I fall unconscious, never to wake up.

The End

44

John Osborne never runs.

Never ran. Until you asked him to.

I crouch against the opposite door, far from the source of leaking gas.

In a five-meter-long tube, far isn't far enough. The invisible gas continues to seep in. I feel groggy. Lightheaded.

Eyelids growing heavy. Can't fight sleep for long. Have time for only one action.

What will it be?

Charge the main exit door and try to knock it down.
Turn to Section 21.

Look for fresh air. Somewhere. Anywhere.
Turn to Section 30.

45

The previous song fades. Another tune takes its place. It sounds slightly older but no less groovy.

More funk. More soul.

Light guitar, bass, keyboard, and drums.

Shoulders swiveling. Body moving.

The singer calls for everybody to hop on the floor and dance!

My hands are on the floor. I spin and twirl. Play Twister with myself.

Reds, greens, blues, and yellows swirl around the room, projected from the spinning balls overhead.

Shake shake shake.

Shake shake shake.

Shake that Osborne boo-tay!

I wipe the sweat from my brow. Johnny's gonna keep dancing 'til the crack of dawn.

A prompt appears on the screen, asking if I'd like to put on the next song.

What do you say?

Yes, please! I can't get enough.
Turn to Section 122.

46

Why am I here? I browse the computer's file directory for files labeled with my name.

Hundreds of folders. Thousands of files.

Search function ... search function ... found it. Here we go. Into the search box I type a single word:

Osborne

Click.

Dozens of files and folders appear. I choose a folder labeled:

Osborne, John

Inside are two documents:

Patient Status

SPEAR Project

Which one should I open first?

Open "Patient Status."
Turn to Section 38.

Open "SPEAR Project."
Turn to Section 50.

47

The first step is to keep my mouth flush against the hole. A strong punch requires a steady oxygen supply.

I rotate my left shoulder back and throw my arm at the door. The punch lands awkwardly — elbow first — leaving a minuscule dent.

A strong punch requires leverage. I suck in a lungful of air and withdraw my mouth from the air hole.

Left arm. Wind up. Knuckle sandwich.

My fist pierces the steel. The force of impact nearly knocks my teeth out. I steady myself and retract my arm.

Punch again. Retract. Breathe. Pummel. Repeat.

Repeat.

Repeat.

Repeat.

Soon the door looks like a slice of Swiss. Gas continues to pour in, contaminating my cache of air. I need to work faster.

I grasp a hole by the rim. The sharp, ragged edge tickles my fingers. I claw at the hole, tearing the steel like it were cardboard.

Groaning, howling, shrieking metal.

I tear until I've merged two small holes into a single larger one. The large gap is wide enough to stick my head through.

I sneak a peek. If the room I'm trapped in were a canary cage, the adjacent room would be a walrus' warehouse. The expansive space is cluttered with tables, trucks, and computers — all sorts of crap.

I take a breath. Retract my head. I'll properly

examine the next room once I'm in it.

I punch more holes. Tear more gaps.

Fists flying. Fingers ripping.

Bruce Lee and Edward Scissorhands had a baby. A baby named John.

Here we go. An opening broad enough to shimmy through.

Jagged metal corners tug at my hospital gown. Yank on my beard. Scratch my skin. Stab at my stomach.

I squeeze through the hole and flop to the floor.

I'm out. I escaped the gas chamber.

I lie prone on the floor of an expansive room. You could fit a hockey rink or two in here. Abandoned military equipment litters the walls and floor.

Lots of gear. No people.

What's next?

Lean against the door and rest for a minute.
Turn to Section 28.

Explore the room immediately.
Turn to Section 120.

"Tell me what I should do later."

Henry smiles pleasantly. "Always looking ahead. Just the kind of forward thinking I've come to expect from the one and only John Osborne. Alrighty, then. Here it is: The key to escaping this complex is to make sure your actions are congruent with how you describe your escape in the future."

"How I describe my escape in the future?" I frown. "How the hell am I supposed to know what I say in the future?"

"You don't, but the person guiding you through *MH-ZERO* should. Assuming they've read *Spear Hunter*, of course. In that novel you briefly summarize your escape to Nathan."

"I see." What a bunch of voodoo mumbo-jumbo. And who is Nathan? "And what if my so-called guide hasn't read *Spear Hunter*?"

"A fair point. Let's just say there's no way you'll get out of here until you cut your hair and trim your beard. *That* is the key."

"Hair and beard. Got it," I say.

Contemplate what to say next.
Turn to Section 77.

49

This room is like a cave.

I'm not a firefly. I need more of the shiny stuff. I select

Lights

Here we go. A single slider lets me brighten or dim all of the building's lights. There are also individual controls for each room.

At the bottom of the control panel is a mysterious button:

DISCO TIME

Disco? Like the dance? And the disco ball?

Ancient stuff. Sounds sketchy.

Do I have the guts to push that button? I'll leave the choice up to you.

Turn up the lights throughout the building.
Turn to Section 37.

Return to the previous menu and figure out how to open the door.
Turn to Section 72.

Press the disco time button and prepare to get down tonight.
Turn to Section 110.

50

SPEAR Project

Inside the folder I find a briefing about my time with the Marines. It's nearly twenty pages long. I scan the important bits.

Dee-dum-dee-do.

Some Marines decided that I was the ideal candidate to receive an experimental replacement arm called SPEAR.

Rum-a-dum-dum-diddle-dee.

Without my knowledge or consent, my superiors decided to forcibly remove my arm and graft a new one in its place. That must be the arm I have now.

Why didn't the Marines just politely ask me if I'd accept an experimental, performance enhancing operation?

They were probably afraid I'd have said no. They would've been right. Replacing an arm is no joke.

I read more.

Biddly-bumbly-bee.

Just as I thought: Given the experimental and non-consensual nature of the operation, the Marines weren't sure how I'd handle it, both physically and psychologically. They wondered how removing my arm without my consent would affect my loyalty. They feared I might desert or seek a discharge.

What brilliant insight. These psychotherapists put my magic eight ball to shame.

Slippity-dippity-doo.

The Marines planned to lie to me. They were gonna disavow all knowledge of the operation and tell me that insurgents had cut off my arm.

Those shit-eating cowards!

My heart races. My fingers tighten around the mouse.

Relax, John. Don't break the mouse. Keep reading. Find out more.

Lickity-slickity-splat-gonna-bash-your-skull-with-a-baseball-bat.

The document goes on to discuss a missing component of my arm — the Northland Core, an experimental power source. In the absence of the Northland Core, a temporary power source is fueling the arm.

A temporary power source. A battery. Estimated lifespan: Five years.

Should the battery die, the bionic arm will tap into my body's metabolism for energy.

No thanks.

Apparently the Northland Core is being developed in another facility.

Where? The document doesn't say.

Experimental surgery? Bionic arm? Northland Core? It's a lot to take in.

What should I do next?

Look at the document called "Patient Status."
Turn to Section 38.

Finish using the computer.
Turn to Section 53.

You're making the right choice.

Shiny chrome scissors in hand, I commence with the clipping. Hair first, then beard.

I grab handfuls of my hair by the roots and cut. I like my hair short — about an inch long. Black strands collect in the sink's basin. By the time I finish delousing myself, the porcelain basin has disappeared.

Already I look more human. Now for the beard.

I've never had a beard before. Never had the opportunity to try growing one while I was in the Marines.

Why not experiment with a little scruff? Could look sexy. And I won't be able to shave myself clean with a scissors, anyway.

I hold the strands of beard near the roots. Trim them with care.

Perfecting my look takes over twenty minutes. When I'm done, a half-inch of black hair covers my jaw and lip.

You certainly are a handsome devil, John Osborne.

I set the scissors aside. Leave a gargantuan mess in the sink.

Back to the hallway. I see two ways to go about this. My gut tells me that this hallway will lead to an exit.

Option one is to hurry. To keep pressing ahead unless something peculiar grabs my attention. Something peculiar like Abe Lincoln snapping a selfie.

Option two is to take my time. Move slowly.

Examine the rooms.

Who knows? Maybe I'll find something useful. A document describing this place. A clue as to what I'm doing down here.

What should I do?

Keep moving forward.
Turn to Section 67.

Take my time and closely examine my surroundings.
Turn to Section 84.

If the corridor I just came from were a stream, this room would be an ocean.

Two trailerless big rigs, an International and a Mack, occupy the center of the room. They're surrounded by wooden pallet crates and an unmarked shipping container. Light posts, like street lamps, provide illumination from the room's edges.

The room is shaped like a parallelogram. Two of the parallel walls are tilted. There's no ceiling to speak of. It's like I'm at the bottom of a sloping tunnel ...

An incline elevator!

I'm standing on a humongous elevator platform. Two sets of tracks run up the lower wall.

I must be deep underground. Jules Verne would be proud.

I step to the edge where the platform meets the tracks. A meter-wide gap separates the platform from the inclined wall.

How many horsepower does it take to lift this platform? Must be a huge motor hiding somewhere nearby.

What should I do next?

Search through the trucks and crates.
Turn to Section 96.

Search for the elevator's controls.
Turn to Section 43.

53

I close the log file. A prompt appears in the middle of the screen:

You have been viewing classified documents. Please enter the appropriate password to confirm your identity.

It asks for a password *after* I've finished looking at the information?

There's nothing to stop me from getting up and walking away. Alternatively, I could try the password I found under the keyboard.

What do you suggest?

Turn and walk away.
Turn to Section 58.

Try keying in "4f5gDser7."
Turn to Section 25.

54

I step back from the door.

What you gonna do now, Miss Disembodied Voice?

Her digital lips remain shut.

I wait five minutes. Nothing happens.

The computer thinks its threat stopped me.

The computer is wrong.

Return to pounding the door as I had been.
Turn to Section 78.

Try to break it down with a single, power-packed punch.
Turn to Section 26.

55

Although I'm tempted to try the elevator, I'd best follow the doctor's advice. His note seemed genuine. He didn't mention the elevator.

Adhering to the good doctor's advice, I head back towards the hallway. On my way to the door, I pass a number of crates.

I'm curious. What do these crates hold? Might be worth a peek.

They're made of wood. Each is held together by hundreds of nails. I don't have a proper tool to open a crate ... but I could blast a few holes into one with this pistol.

What do you say?

The crates look hungry. Feed them some lead.
Turn to Section 104.

Keep moving.
Turn to Section 107.

56

I stretch my fingers across the hand reader. Again, the blue light sweeps from top to bottom.

A message appears on the screen:

PLEASE WAIT.

A low hum reverberates nearby.

Could be the door's mechanism.

Could be something malicious.

The buzz picks up speed. Grows louder.

Something doesn't seem right. What should I do?

Hold tight and see what happens.
Turn to Section 111.

Remove my palm.
Turn to Section 98.

57

Is that your best idea?
    Seriously?
    You don't deserve to witness

The End

58

I get up and walk away from the computer. These computer programmers ought to reconsider their security protocol.

Something whirs behind me. Probably the computer's fan. Nothing to —

BANG!

The End

59

I turn away from my family and friends.

It's not time for me to join them. Not yet.

I walk into the darkness, away from the tunnel of light.

Jogging.

Running.

Sprinting.

I'm surrounded by black upon black. Darkness upon darkness.

Wait. There is something. A vague shape in the distance. A man lying on thin air.

Me.

Continue to next page.

The other me is all alone, still in the hospital gown, unconscious. He has wild, unruly hair and a Moses beard. He rests at my waist level, as though sleeping on an invisible table.

What happened?

My head. Something hard. It seemed like a good idea at the time.

I feel the other me's forehead. He's warm. Feverish.

He stirs ever so slightly.

I feel myself dissipating. Disintegrating. Becoming one with the other, unconscious me.

The other me vanishes.

I see only black.

My eyes flutter open. I'm in the corridor, on my back. The ceiling glares down at me.

I sit up. Rise to my feet.

Um ... how about we take a closer look at that main exit door?

Examine the main exit door.
Turn to Section 14.

60

You're right. This place looks abandoned. Why not toss away the basic laws of human hygiene and piss wherever I damn please?

Unbound by societal constraints, I step into another corner and lift my hospital gown. A moment later a yellow stream spouts forth.

It reminds me of a song by one of those gloomy British bands. I think it went something like:

> *Look at the cars*
> *Look how they honk at you*
> *And all the things you do*
> *And they were taxi yellow*

> *You sing a song*
> *You sing a song for stew*
> *And all the stew beef, too*
> *And the sauce was yellow*

> *So then I dropped trou*
> *And said let's do this now*
> *And it exploded yellow*

Hmm ... I think I flubbed a line or two.

The liquid pools in the corner. Little rivulets trickle back in my direction. They grow wider and longer, running across the floor, seeping under the computer console. I step to avoid them.

I finish and let my hospital gown drop.

How convenient. Now I understand why the Irish wear kilts. I turn to walk away.

Yucccck. A lukewarm, wet feeling under my bare

foot.

Dammit.

Well, one dirty foot deserves another. Besides, I've heard that the yellow stuff is a powerful disinfectant. Who knows what's been growing on my feet while I was out.

My second foot touches the pool. A painful tingling sensation overwhelms my body.

Shaking. Convulsing. My limbs are lost to me.

The lights go out.

Black.

Free from the electrical surge, I collapse to the floor.

Something feels wrong. Very wrong.

Dizzy. Lightheaded. Like I can't breathe. I reach to my chest.

Lungs are working. Heart isn't.

No pulse. No heart, no oxygen. The liquid must've come into contact with a loose wire. Created a short circuit.

I was electrocuted by my own piss.

I remain pathetically splayed out on the floor. Soon I fall unconscious.

I never wake up.

The End

Exit, please.

I trace the room's outer edge, pacing past the rows of lockers. The wall soon deposits me before a two-paneled door, tall and wide enough for an FMTV to drive through. Yellow letters spell:

EXIT

The seam between the door panels splits the letters into pairs.

Beside the door is a hand scanner. Must be electronically locked. I doubt I'm authorized to open it. Still, it might be worth a try.

Try the hand scanner.
Turn to Section 70.

Rummage through the lockers instead.
Turn to Section 114.

62

I examine the note. The letters are printed. Clear and legible. I read.

Dear John,

A love letter to me? How did this guy know I'd be the one to find it?

You are one stubborn bastard, Osborne. You know that? How many years are you planning to lie there, comatose?

I'm sick of waiting. Sick of eating reconstituted food. Sick of never seeing the sun. Sick of being alone.

So I'm giving up. If you wake up eventually, great. If not, well, frankly I couldn't give a shit anymore.

I think you'll do fine without me. Besides, even if you did wake up, I would still be stuck here. The virus lingers topside, and I don't have immunity. If I go outside, I die. (Honestly, I'm surprised that the quarantine here has held up this long. No carrier organisms have managed to penetrate the seal — at least not as of this writing.)

Carrier organism? Virus? I can see why he wouldn't want to go outside. Maybe I won't want to go out either.

You, on the other hand, should do perfectly fine. In fact, that's part of the reason why you were selected to receive the SPEAR — because you happened to be born with immunity to a number of artificial viruses. Lucky you.

Good news: Sounds like I can go outside.

Bad news: I have no idea what SPEAR is. And this virus talk is creeping me out.

Anyway, you've been asleep for quite some time now. (If the Pentagon had foreseen you'd be out this long, they never would've signed off on your operation. Of that much I'm sure.) If and when you get out, you'll discover a world nothing like the one you remember. I haven't been able to explore it for myself — save for the occasional excursion in a hazmat suit — so I can only imagine.

Let me guess: You're wondering how to get out of here. The safest and most direct way out is to walk down the long, long path. If you happen upon any locked doors, don't be shy about using the SPEAR. Keep going and eventually you'll arrive at an exit.

Good luck. You're gonna need it.

Yours truly,

Dr. Doctor

P.S. I'm not sure who you'll run into topside. I imagine Colonel Stearns is up there somewhere. For what it's worth, he believed he was acting in your best interest.

I've been out for a long time? How long? And what is this about Colonel Stearns? This note is like a hackneyed plot device from a bad science fiction movie.

Invasion of the SPEAR Hunters 3: Viral Outbreak vs. Reconstituted Food

I reach down to the floor mat and pick up the doctor's SIG Sauer pistol. It's a P226, a variant common amongst law enforcement.

You never know when a little firepower could come in handy.

I hop out of the truck's cabin. My bare feet smack the elevator platform's cold, hard floor. What's next?

Follow the man's instructions and head down the corridor.
Turn to Section 55.

Try to make this platform lift me up and outta here.
Turn to Section 22.

63

I hoist the keyboard above my head. I wanna chuck it across the room. Smash it into cockroach kibble.

Huh? What's that?

A small slip of paper is taped to the keyboard's underside. There's something written on it.

4f5gDser7

I replace the keyboard on the desk. Let's pretend that outburst never happened.

I punch in the password and hit enter. The blinking cursor disappears.

Welcome!

Christ. I never would've guessed that password. Apparently not even the computer techs could remember it. Hence the note.

The screen brings up a desktop full of icons. A familiar interface. What should I look for?

Look for information about why I'm here.
Turn to Section 46.

Try to find out how to get outta here.
Turn to Section 118.

Search for snippets of salaciously saucy cinema.
Turn to Section 29.

Turn off the computer and try the door instead.
Turn to Section 9.

64

I sit on the floor. Lean against the wall. Wait.

Silence.

Utter silence.

I lay myself out across the metal floor. All that running made me tired.

It's chilly. The hospital gown lets the stale air get intimate with my skivvies. On the bright side, my over-sized bird's nest of hair makes a comfy pillow.

Hours pass.

No one comes.

No one will.

What's next?

Wait longer. Help is surely on the way. Surely!
Turn to Section 91.

Stand up and carefully examine the main exit door.
Turn to Section 14.

Use my head as a battering ram to hit the door.
Turn to Section 42.

65

I click a button labeled:

Cameras, Sensors, and Automated Defense
Systems

A prompt asks me for a password. I could try the same password I used previously. Lots to gain and nothing to lose, if you ask me.

Or I can consider other options. Your choice.

Enter the password "4f5gDser7."
Turn to Section 123.

Return to the previous menu and
try to open the door.
Turn to Section 72.

Return to the previous menu and
see if I can turn up the lights.
Turn to Section 49.

Give in to your delirium, John. Let it sweep you away.

I nod weakly.

"I'll set you back just a few minutes," the voice says. "I trust you'll make the right choice this time."

I nod again. My mind disconnects from my body. My consciousness is tugged from my corporeal form.

My outer shell lies dying. My inner being drifts through the air. The next thing I know I'm looking down at myself from above.

My other self stands at a hand scanner, his right hand on the panel.

An irresistible force stuffs my consciousness into my other self's body. I'm a pillow being forced into too small a case.

Then it's over.

I blink. A line of red text comes into focus.

SCANNING ERROR. PLEASE TRY AGAIN.

I feel inexplicably compelled to put my left hand on the scanner.

Try my left hand.
Turn to Section 88.

67

This hallway is getting me down. The walls may as well be blue. Blue steel.

Let's move as quickly as possible. If I don't find the exit at the corridor's end, I can double back and examine everything more thoroughly.

I break into a light jog. Bare feet on metallic floor.

Doors lead into bland operating rooms, identical to the two I already visited.

The room numbers count down towards zero.

70.

46.

25.

11.

5.

A doorway opens directly ahead. I keep jogging. Keep steady.

Go through the open doorway.
Turn to Section 24.

I browse the file system. I need more information about this facility.

Experiment results

Spider Solitaire

Cat videos

SPEAR specs

Minesweeper

Nothing useful. A warning appears on screen:

Low battery. Please reconnect to an external power source immediately.

I groan. This rig is running on batteries? I frantically scour the file tree.

Found it!

Security Control Panel

My cursor hovers over the file.

Battery critical. Shutting down now.

No!

Black screen. Not even enough battery left for a proper shutdown.

That was fruitless. Thanks a lot, Little John.

Looks like I'll have to try the door.

Go to the door.
Turn to Section 9.

69

You never know what a locker might hide. Big guns? Large knives? A stash of raunchy magazines?

I walk the row of lockers, checking the locks. About a dozen lockers down I find another unlocked one.

I pry the door open. The main compartment is empty. I reach up to feel the top shelf. My hand discovers a leathery object, coiled like a rope.

Standing on my tiptoes for a better look, I cross eyes with a snake. The scaly reptile sticks out its tongue and hisses.

It launches at my neck. Fangs penetrate my throat.

I stumble to the floor. Struggle to breathe.

Poisonous venom? A hole in my windpipe?

The diamond-backed snake slithers from the locker. I flail at it as it approaches. Already my strength is fading.

The reptile wraps around my throat. Tightens its grip. Chokes off my windpipe.

I can only imagine the vibrant colors my face must be turning.

The End

70

I flatten my right hand on the scanner. A blue fluorescent light appears. It scans my hand from top to bottom.

An LED display flashes to life with words in red: SCANNING ERROR. PLEASE TRY AGAIN.

Hmm ...

I don't see what I could've done wrong. I could try again, or I could look elsewhere.

Try the scanner again.
Turn to Section 56.

Peruse the nearby lockers.
Turn to Section 114.

71

I ignore the voice. I don't fear death.

"I understand," the voice says. "Better luck next time, John."

I lie alone. My life comes to a solemn close.

An unsettling sensation overwhelms me. A sense that maybe, just maybe, this isn't how my story was supposed to turn out in

The End

72

Open the door. Gotta open the door. Hell, maybe I can open all the doors.

Hmm ... looks like I'm in luck:

Open All Doors.

I give it a solid click.

Clank, clank, clank, clank.

The sound of heavy steel doors opening in succession. The crashes and clangs continue for the span of a deep breath.

The echoes dissipate. Silence prevails.

Eerie silence.

Should I venture into the hallway? Or should I examine the security settings further?

Leave now.
Turn to Section 18.

Fiddle with the computer's security settings.
Turn to Section 4.

Johnny's a good boy.

I leave the SIG on the floor. Walk over to the restraining table. Sit on it. The table's thin padding doesn't offer much cush for my pantsless tush. And to think, I was lying on one of these for years.

I wait silently. My stomach growls. I haven't eaten since I woke up.

5 minutes.

10 minutes?

20 minutes? I've had enough.

I march up to the door. Pound on it ferociously.

"How about you get me some dinner in here?"

No one answers my scream. Not even an echo. The room is a sonic dead zone.

For kicks, I switch arms and beat the door again.

Bam!

Before any dry sarcastic taunts can escape my mouth, I stop.

There's a dent in the door. My fist left a huge impression in the door. Did I my left hand just make a crater in the steel?

Holy shit. No wonder it was so easy for my left arm to break free of its restraints.

That note in the truck mentioned I could use SPEAR to get through doors. SPEAR must be my arm.

It makes sense. I lost my arm. I was given a weaponized replacement. In fact, that must be the whole reason I'm down here.

Now I need to get out. I slam the door with my left hand again. It gives a little further.

"Please remain calm and wait for the appropriate personnel to come to your assistance," a voice announces. "Do not try to escape, or I will have no choice but to respond with lethal force."

No one is coming to my assistance. There's only one way out. I pound the door again and again. The craters in its surface deepen. It won't hold up for long.

A bang rattles my ears.

Not the bang of my fist on the door. The bang of gunfire.

Pain. Skull-rending pain. The threat of lethal force was no joke.

My final fleeting thought is that somehow, in another life, I will escape this place. I will escape this hellhole.

The End

Right branch it is. I run ahead.

I sprint past doors and windows, like the ones I just escaped. No time to explore.

My bare feet pound against the metal floor. The alarm wails like nukes are about to drop. The crimson warning lights throb.

A dull, resonant thump emanates from behind me. I look back.

Nothing. Only darkness.

I run. Thirty seconds pass.

A minute. Three minutes.

The corridor seems to angle slightly upward. Am I underground?

Six minutes. Still running.

Ten minutes? Twelve minutes? I'm not sure.

Finally I spot the end. I slow to a halt before a metal door, smooth as polished stone.

MAIN EXIT

Good to know. But how do I get through?

I lean on the door. Panting. Heaving.

Another resounding thud sounds behind me. I spin around. A blast door has come down, cutting me off from the way I came.

That's what the thumping was. Dropping doors.

The alarm system falls silent. The pulsating red lights are replaced by a steady white fluorescent glow.

I'm trapped in a section of corridor about five meters long.

A pleasant female voice announces through the speakers: "Please remain calm and wait for the appropriate personnel to come to your assistance."

Assistance? I'm not buying it. Based on what I've seen, the staff here doesn't have my best interests in mind ... not that I've seen any staff. What the hell happened here? Where is everyone?

Focus, John. Escape first. Question later.

This closed-off section of corridor is like a metal tube. The ceiling looms a couple feet above my head. No windows. Only two hulking steel doors.

It'll take more than my fists to bust free.

I see two options.

You choose.

Wait for a knight in shining armor to come save me.
Turn to Section 64.

Examine the door labeled MAIN EXIT.
Turn to Section 14.

"What inspired you to create me?" I ask.

A grin spreads across Henry's face. "Impressive. Despite being strapped to a table, unsure of where he is and how he'll escape, John Osborne still finds time to humor me with a personal question. That's Sean-Connery-as-James-Bond-level courage. Courage that would make Bruce Willis and Nicholas Cage green with envy."

"Thanks for the psychoanalysis, Freud."

"My pleasure! Anyhow, *The Northland Chronicles* came to me as I was sitting in the back of a car, heading home from camping in the Boundary Waters Canoe Area. Watching the scenery pass by, I was struck by how little the end of the world would affect northern Minnesota. This realization drove me to create a post-apocalyptic setting. Once the background was in place, I then drafted you, John Osborne, to play the jaded hero. By the time I arrived home the Chronicles were set to begin. I dropped everything I was working on and started writing your story. The rest, as they say, is history."

Continue to next page.

"So I was conceived in a tent during a camping trip," I say.

Henry clears his throat. "After the camping trip, to be precise."

Seems I have time for another question. What'll it be?

Ask Henry about what he plans to write next.
Turn to Section 109.

Ask him a more personal question.
Turn to Section 93.

76

I offer my palm to the panel a second time. I'm suddenly struck by the fineness of my hands. Perfectly proportioned. Strong fingers. Not too hairy. Maybe I should look for work as a hand model.

The blue light does its dance. When it finishes scanning, a message appears:

PLEASE WAIT.

I hear a dull buzz. A whine in my ear. The sound grows and grows. Soon it resembles the growl of an electric drill.

I purse my lips. I have a bad feeling about this.

Before I can remove my hand, two steel crescents shoot from the scanning machine. They clasp my wrist like a bracelet. Like a handcuff.

My hand. My gorgeous hand! If anything happens —

A surge of high-voltage electricity courses through my arm.

Heat builds within my body. Cooks me from the inside out.

I fall to my knees. Hit the floor hard. The last thing I smell is the stench of charred flesh.

Johnny Storm I am not.

The End

I'm about to ask another question when Henry opens his big trap.

"Anyway, I'm afraid I must return to my desk and finish writing this story. Hordes of expectant readers are eagerly awaiting this adventure!"

"You're gonna leave me here?"

"Well, yes and no," Henry says with a smile that transcends adverbial wordiness. "I'm going to send you back to the beginning of this mess. Unfortunately, I'm afraid you won't have any memory of this meeting. I can't allow my star creation to become cognizant of his fictional nature."

"Why talk with me if I won't remember?"

"*You* won't remember, but the *reader* will. Hopefully they'll make better choices next time around. Now, close your eyes."

"Close my eyes? Is this kindergarten?"

"No. But I certainly could pen a novel called *Northland Kindergarten: John's Big Day Out,* if you'd like. I fear sales would be dreadful, however."

"Whatever," I grunt.

I close my eyes. My consciousness evaporates into the air.

I'm leaving my body. Circling around the room. Slipping back into my physical self.

Groggy. Lying on something hard.

Sore back. Achy neck.

Where am I?

Wake up and find out.
Turn to Section 1.

78

I'm still not sure what to make of this this left arm. Don't wanna push it too hard. For all I know it's powered by a miniature nuclear reactor.

Chernobyl. Fukushima. Yongbyon. John Osborne's bionic limb.

I return to pounding the door at a steady clip. The pleasant female voice returns.

Stop immediately or face the consequences. Yadda yadda yadda.

The door will give sooon. I caan feeel it.

Eh?

I stop punching. Gotta recalibrate my center of gravity.

What's that hissing sound?

Gas?

Since when? I couldn't hear over my pounding.

Yawn.

Sleeeepy.

I want to lie doown. But I shouldn't ...

Don't sleep, John.

Eyelids heavvy. Soo heaavy.

STAY AWAKE!

Huhhh? What waaaaas that? Meeeee?

FIGHT IT, JOHN!

But whyyyyy? Sweeeeeeep is gooood.

A little naaaaap couldn't hurd, riiiiighd?

I'll wag ub sooon. Ged baaaag do ... whadeba id was ......

Ebweeding weel wooowwwwg ouud in ...

The End

This door is big. Bigger than the one I punched through to escape the gas chamber. Still, the same principals should apply. Beat at it long enough and I'll break through.

I choose a spot near the center. The seam where the two panels meet should be the weak point.

I punch. The steel gives.

Three punches later I've bored my first hole. This won't take long.

Pummel the steel. Make a hole. Rip it wider. Bore my way to freedom.

Sunshine

Grass.

Trees.

I see them through the hole.

Within another minute I've clawed open a jagged cavity that's big enough to slide through. I toss my gun out the hole, then clamber through.

My palms hit dirt. A dirt road, overgrown with grass and weeds. It leads away from building, into a forest.

A forest? This definitely isn't Egypt. Judging from the trees and shrubs, it's probably Europe or the United States. Maybe the Midwest or Appalachia.

Behind me is a steep, rocky hillside. Inset in the weather-stained rocks is the steel door.

MH-0

MH? Marine Hospital? Military Hospital?

Two dark chrome panels set in a hill, and three mysterious letters. Awfully unassuming considering what's inside. If I were a lost hiker, I'd guess this was an old mine, sealed off and abandoned.

I'd best abandon it, too. I set off along the road.

Fresh air. Bright sun. I'm deep in the wilderness. Hopefully not too deep. I need to find someone with a telephone. Got calls I need to —

CRACK!

Sharp pain in my back. Mind-rending pressure in my chest. I stumble forward.

I've been shot. By who?

I fall to my knees. Blood gushes from the wound. My hospital gown oozes red.

I struggle for air.

Two men dash toward me. Two men with rifles.

I collapse just as they reach me.

"Desolation! It's a man! I thought it was sumkinda monster." The man takes a knee beside me. "Been years since I a-seen a wild beard like this feller's."

"What the hell we gon' do now?"

"You tell me. Yer the one who up and shot him."

"Only 'cause you told me ta! Said you a-seen a bearded monster!"

"Well, now you know you oughta not listen ta me."

"Yer fulla shit. Desolation, I knew you was a-talking crazy, saying you'd a-spotted a radiation monster. We both know thems monsters ain't real. Just a myth ta keep youngins outta the fallout areas."

I try to choke out a few words.

"Looky! He's a-trying to say sumthin'!" the kneeling man says.

"What's he sayin'?" the standing man asks.

My lips move. No words come out.

Eyes close.

"I think we're a-losin' him."

"All yer fault, buddy. Next time you'd best a-looky before you shoot. Just 'cause we shave ever-day don't mean a man can't grow himself a mean-lookin' beard."

Consciousness slips away. This must be

The End

A grenade is worth a thousand bullets.

I reach for my belt. Unclip a grenade. I pull the pin and roll it towards the exit. It clinks across the floor. I dash to take cover behind an FMTV.

Two. One. Boom!

Krakatoa in a canister.

A shock wave reverberates through the room. The FMTV rocks back and forth on its wheels, nearly knocking me to the floor.

I hear shattering glass. A twinge of pain hits my chest. The pain passes quickly, as though it was never there.

I wait behind the truck. Ears still ringing, I rise to my feet.

A black pattern, like soot marks on the bottom of a pot, mars the door. A surface stain. No sign of structural damage.

Damn.

Another stab of pain wracks my heart. I clutch my chest.

Warm. Sticky.

Blood. Fresh blood on my hand. The blood seeps through my fatigues, staining them dark red.

Gushing blood. Minimal pain. I've heard stories of this of phenomenon. I can think of only one explanation: A fragment of shrapnel must've hit me straight in the heart.

The grenade shattered the windows of all three trucks. Did a shard cut through me and transfix my ticker?

Feeling woozy and weak, I lie down. No reason to make my heart fight gravity. Though I'm a goner,

I might last a minute or two longer if I calm myself.

Freedom. Freedom was so close.

What was outside? Were my friends and family waiting for me?

I close my eyes. It won't be long now. I hover on the fringes of consciousness.

A voice whispers in my ear:

"John, would you like another chance?"

A hallucination. An artifact of my dying brain trying to assuage my fears.

"I'll give you one more chance, John. If you want it, it's yours."

It's a man's voice. I don't recognize it. But he sounds friendly enough.

What should I do?

Accept the offer.
Turn to Section 66.

Ignore the voice.
Turn to Section 71.

81

Getting out of here would be good. Getting out of here intact would be better.

I sprint towards the door. Sidestep around the table.

A red laser beam extends past the side of my head. A bead appears on the far wall.

The bead disappears. Red One to Mission Control: Target locked-in.

I duck and weave. The laser reappears above my head, like a red thread leading out the doorway.

A report of gunfire. A whoosh through my hair.

Move!

I crouch lower. Speed up. Dash through the door into the hallway.

Another blast rattles my eardrums. I dive left, taking cover beside the door frame. I should be safe here, outside the gun's line of sight.

I crawl ahead, keeping below the windows. Where the row of windows ends the corridor veers right. I rise to my feet and hurry around the corner.

I find an open door. I'm lucky my bogus password didn't trigger a facility-wide lockdown.

The door leads into an expansive-looking room. Let's take a look inside.

Enter the big room.
Turn to Section 52.

Maybe you're onto something. Having a little fun couldn't hurt. All work, no play ... you know.

I leap out of the truck. Roar with delight. Start unloading the M27's magazine.

The clip is about half empty when a ricocheting bullet nails me above the left ear.

Through my skull. Out the right side of my jaw.

Not that I'm aware of any of this. I'm brain dead before my body hits the floor.

Ignorance is bliss.

Thanks.

The End

83

I'm in no mood for a long, contemplative stroll. Besides, I may as well poke my head around this corner, seeing as it's so close. Who knows? Maybe this is where the leprechaun hides his lucky charms.

I go left. Dim fluorescent bulbs overhead light my way. The entire corridor — walls, floor, and ceiling — seems to be made of stainless steel. This place wasn't built on the cheap.

I take a few steps. Turn right at the sharp corner. Stand before a door frame. It leads into what appears to be a vast room.

I step through.

Examine this new room.
Turn to Section 52.

No harm in taking my time to escape.

I stroll down the hall. Pop into a few rooms. I find bottles of pills. Syringes. Medicine vials.

Painkillers. Psychotropics. Bizarrely named medications.

Blaxiflaph. Hormonogrow. MHP-173.

You won't find these pharmaceuticals in your neighborhood drugstore. Some of the bottles have expiration dates, ranging from 2027 to 2035.

I pass more operating rooms. I notice that there's no Room 100. The room numbers skip from 99 to 101.

Is there a hospital taboo I don't know about? Americans are wary of thirteen. East Asians associate the number four with death. I've never heard of any superstitions surrounding the big one-oh-oh.

Why the missing room? Maybe the answer lies just beyond my reach ...

I continue down the hallway. Pass room 50 on my right. Room 25 comes on my left. Around the time I reach room 10, I discern the faint outline of a doorway ahead.

Keep moving forward.
Turn to Section 24.

85

EXIT

I see potential here.

The door has two panels, split vertically. If they were to slide apart, an FMTV could drive right through.

Adjacent to the door is a hand scanner. Though I doubt my palm will work, it's worth a try.

I rest my right hand on the scanner. A bright, whitish-blue light sweeps from the top of the panel to the bottom.

Red texts appears above the scanner:

SCANNING ERROR. PLEASE TRY AGAIN.

Odd. The scanner looked like it was working fine.

Let's give it another go. Right hand or left?

Try my right hand again.
Turn to Section 76.

Switch to my left.
Turn to Section 88.

I notch the M27 against my shoulder. Spin one-eighty. Drop to a knee.

Strange. There's no one behind me. Is my imagination toying with me?

All search and no shoot makes John a dull boy.

I know I heard something. I'd better hang onto this gun. Just in case.

Decide what to do next.
Turn to Section 119.

Grenades, vests, pistols, assault rifles. The tables have it all.

I lock eyes on a hefty Desert Eagle semi-automatic. Pick it up. Appreciate how it fits my hand.

Feels damn good.

I eject the magazine. It's still loaded. I slam it back into the magazine tube and slip the gun into my holster. I also clip a couple of grenades to my belt. You never know when you'll need a little extra heat.

I leave the bulletproof vests. I don't want to lug around the extra weight.

As I peruse the tables, I catch sight of a door. Its metallic panels features a single word in bright yellow paint:

EXIT

Looks promising. I didn't see it until now because the FMTVs had been blocking my view. Speaking of which ...

Scope out the door.
Turn to Section 85.

Circle back to check out the trucks.
Turn to Section 103.

It's lefty's turn to step up to the plate.

But first a precaution. My right hand draws my new best friend, the Desert Eagle, from its holster.

Protection in case I trip an alarm. Defense against whatever awaits outside.

I splay my left hand's fingers across the panel. The blue light reappears. Scans my hand from top to bottom.

Red characters appear above the scanner:
PLEASE WAIT.

I hear a faint hum, like the buzz of a small motor.

Please wait for what? For the door to open?

The hum grows. Revs higher. Builds into a throaty, chainsaw-like growl.

Something's not right.

Two metal crescents leap from the scanner. They lock together over my wrist, shackling my arm in place.

Looks like I'm not supposed to leave during the performance.

The roar grows louder and louder. Like a jet engine in my ears. A jet engine that wants to chew me up and spit me out.

Flashes of electricity, miniature lightning bolts, surge across the cuff. All through the electric light show, I feel only a dull tingling in my wrist.

The metal restrain glows red. Vermilion. Like magma.

Why isn't the bracelet scorching my hand? Why isn't the electric current flowing into my body?

Why am I not trying to escape?

I yank my left arm away from the panel. My wrist

slices through the cuff like a laser beam through a Hershey's bar, cutting a gap in the metal.

I stumble backwards. My ass hits the floor hard.

That was easy.

I stagger to my feet. Rub my sore rear end. Whatever voodoo magic protected my wrist doesn't cover my ass.

As I'm gathering my wits, the panel explodes. Pieces of shrapnel zip through the room. I shield my eyes with my forearm.

Continue to next page.

A second later, all falls silent. I cautiously lower my arm. From the broken panel rises a column of smoke.

Victory is mine. If only I knew how I won.

My left arm. It's definitely not the arm Momma Osborne gave me. It must be a replacement of some kind ... a replacement that's heatproof and what else?

I slip the Desert Eagle back into its holster — I'd forgotten it was in my other hand — and inspect the panel's smoldering remains. The hand-scanning surface is cracked. A gaping hole exposes the circuitry within. I think it's read its last palm.

A robotic female voice announces through speakers overhead:

"Damage to security systems detected. Please remain calm and wait for the appropriate personnel to come to your assistance."

Fat chance, lady. This is my game. We'll play my way.

Use heavy weaponry to blow a hole in the door.
Turn to Section 80.

Backtrack into the facility and
look for an exit elsewhere.
Turn to Section 117.

Pound on the door in frustration.
Turn to Section 106.

"So, Mr. Wise Guy. You say you created me — that this is just a story. If that's the case, you should know everything about me, past and present. So tell me: what's the deal with my arm? I thought I lost it. Now it's back."

Henry grins mischievously. "Funny you should ask. In fact, your arm happens to be the focus of *The Northland Chronicles.* I don't want to spoil anything for you. All I'll say is that your memories about your arm are accurate: You did lose it in combat, and the limb hanging from your left shoulder now is indeed a replacement."

"That's all you got for me?"

Henry scratches his chin. "Well, I suppose sharing a bit more couldn't hurt. What do you want to know?"

Let's consider this carefully. I've never seen a replacement arm that looks so real. What should I ask?

Ask if there's anything special about the arm.
Turn to Section 16.

Ask why not every wounded soldier gets
a true-to-life replacement arm.
Turn to Section 11.

A door I can dent is a door I can break.

I take a deep breath. Wind my arm back. Send my fist on a collision course with the steel.

Crunch. Like punching tinfoil.

Clang. Bang. Clank. A fresh crater with each hit.

An impassive voice lectures overhead:

"Please remain calm and wait for the appropriate personnel to come to your assistance. Do not try to escape, or I will have no choice but to respond with lethal force."

I hesitate. The building is vacant. What good is a threat with no one to back it up? Does this computer have automated means of applying its so-called lethal force?

I eye the pattern of dents. The door won't hold much longer.

I clench my teeth and ready my fist. The assault continues.

Mr. Door, you'll soon be no more.

Between the thumps of my fist against metal, I hear a subtle hiss, like air escaping from a blow-up mattress.

The air overhead shimmers. A stream of gas leaking in.

What flavor of gas? I'd rather skip the taste test, thanks.

I punch faster. Increase my volume without sacrificing power. This arm seemingly has no limits.

The gas starts to hit me.

Drowsy. An unsettling sense of calm.

I gotta keep working. Like a diesel engine's piston, my arm fires again and again. My fist penetrates the steel. My arm careens forward until the hole has engulfed the entire limb.

Gas continues to hiss. I extract my arm and continue punching. I beat the steel. Make the gap wider and wider.

Finally the hole is big enough to shimmy through. Using my fist like a mallet, I hammer down the sharp, jagged edges.

I climb through headfirst. Brace my palms on the opposite floor. Drag myself through. Flop to freedom.

I'm back in the expansive sky-lit room. I never should've left. After a moment's rest I hop to my feet. The poisonous gas is nasty stuff — some kind of narcotic — and it's seeping into this room through the hole I just made. This isn't a good place to take a breather.

Gotta push forward. My walloping left arm will punch my ticket out of here.

Should I pummel my way through the main door ASAP? Or should I scrounge up more supplies before I leave?

Head for the exit immediately.
Turn to Section 101.

Search for useful supplies.
Turn to Section 113.

Okay. I'll wait here.

Gonna close my eyes and take a little nap.

I wake up a while later. Nothing's changed.

I try meditating. But I was never much good at that Zen hullabaloo. Soon I drift to sleep again. Sometimes I roll onto my side. Change things up a bit. I never bother getting to my feet. Too much work.

I repeat this process for what must be days.

Parched throat. Sulky stomach. Growing weak.

But you know what? You told me to wait here. So I'm gonna wait. Wait until help comes. Because obviously you, dear reader, know something that John Osborne doesn't.

And there you have it. John Osborne is now referring to himself in the third person.

Is this what you wanted? For John Osborne to lose his marbles and waltz through the burning wreckage of the fourth wall?

John Osborne lies on the floor. He never gets up again. He dies there in that lonely corridor.

Does anyone ever find John Osborne's body?

How would he know? He's dead.

The End

The FMTVs seem promising. I head to the closest one, its bed covered by a sloped canvas roof. Peeking inside, I find only empty benches. No men, no gear.

To the cabin! The driver-side door is unlocked. I let myself in. Check the ignition.

A thumb reader? I'd forgotten the Marines were phasing out flip-switch ignitions. These newer thumb-activated ignitions are a pain in the ass to jump-start.

I search the cabin. Nothing of note inside.

I hop out. Two trucks left. No reason to check them in order. I walk past the nearer one. Continue to the one further away.

I like variety. Ketchup one day, Tabasco the next.

The bed of the far truck is as barren as the first. The cabin proves slightly more promising. Near the steering wheel is an old-fashioned starter.

Bingo. Let's rev her up. I try the switch.

Nothing. Not even a token effort to turn over. Battery must be dead.

I give the cabin a once over. The only object of interest is a green cap. Stitched onto its front panel is a single word:

MARINES

I try it on. Hopefully the previous owner was acquainted with Head & Shoulders.

I glance at myself in the rear-view mirror. I gotta say, since trimming my facial hair I look pretty slick. But the green cap doesn't suit me. I flip it off my head and toss it onto the seat.

I step out. Move onto the final truck.

Empty cargo bed. Nondescript cabin. Starter switch.

I try firing it up. Silence. Not even a flicker of life.

I slip out of the cabin. Smack my lips in disappointment.

I could try jump-starting the first rig, the one with the thumb-scanning ignition. But it's likely just as a dead as the other two.

There are better ways to spend my time. What should I do?

Look for an exit.
Turn to Section 61.

Search the wall lockers.
Turn to Section 114.

Take a closer look at the equipment on the tables.
Turn to Section 99.

93

A more personal question? Let's see ...

"What's your favorite food?"

Henry gives me a quizzical look. It seems I've pitched him a curve ball.

A little-league curve ball.

"That's a good question. When I was younger I was a picky eater. I'd eat ketchup-only hamburgers, unadorned cheese pizza, and boring vanilla ice cream. My particular eating habits drove my parents into paroxysms of rage," Henry says, his eyes glazing over with nostalgia. "Over the last five or six years, however, I've branched out. I'd now say my favorite food is fried rice. Korean-style kimchi and pork fried rice is especially delicious."

"Can't say I've tried it."

"I know. I created you, remember?"

"So you say." I'm still not buying it.

Ask another question.
Turn to Section 77.

I set the gun down. Raise my hands above my head. Swivel around.

I lock eyes with a white male. Average height. Black t-shirt and blue jeans. A stubbly beard.

Unarmed. Definitely not military.

"Hi there, John. It's good to see you."

"Do I know you?"

"You don't. But I know you."

"That right?" I raise an eyebrow.

"Let's just say I've been keeping an eye on you. You're a rather important part of my life." The man smiles proudly.

"Huh," I grunt. "I see."

"Anyway, I have bad news: You aren't supposed to be here — at least not yet"

"Oh yeah?" I cross my arms.

"With the help of your bookish friend — the one watching over your shoulder — you've progressed further and faster than I'd imagined you could."

I level this guy with a cold, hard stare. I have no clue what he's babbling about.

"By arriving here without first accomplishing other necessary tasks, you have broken the continuity of *The Northland Chronicles*. That is to say that the John Osborne you are at present has diverged significantly from the John Osborne that's supposed to appear in *A Stranger North*."

Could I get that again, *en inglés?*

The man, as though reading my thoughts, continues: "What does that mean for you? It means that I can't let you escape, John. Not in your present condition."

"Can't let me escape?" I clench my fists. "What the hell do you mean?"

The man shrugs. "Well, in fact you're free to leave. But I guarantee it won't end well."

I grit my teeth. Won't end well? We'll see about that.

"I propose a compromise," the man says. "I'll let you return to the opening scene. You'll wake up on that table with no memory of this encounter. But the helper hovering above your shoulder *will* remember, and this time he or she will make better decisions and guide you out of here without a hitch."

What a buncha voodoo mumbo jumbo. But I think I understand.

Continue to next page.

"So, let me get this straight." I reach to rub my chin but end up with a handful of beard instead. This tangled mass of beard could house a family of gerbils. "You're saying that if I leave this building now I'll disrupt the future, but it's okay for me to go back in time and start again?"

"That's the gist of it," the man says, nodding amicably.

"Mind giving me a second to think about this?"

"Not at all. Take all the time you need."

Questions: Who is this guy? What is he doing here?

Questions. No answers.

Can he really send me back a few hours? If I ask, he'll probably respond with more rambling time-travel twaddle.

This is a matter of faith. Faith in a nutjob.

Do I want to abandon my progress and start again?

Accept the man's offer to return to the beginning.
Turn to Section 31.

Reach to the table behind me for a gun.
Turn to Section 105.

95

I snatch the SIG from the floor and hop to my feet.

Nothing happens. Maybe the security system can't recognize that I've picked up the pistol.

Maybe it has no means to enforce its threats.

Maybe it's taking measures against me discreetly.

I step to the windows. Retreat a couple feet. Clutch the SIG in both hands.

I fire two rounds into the glass. The bullets flatten out, lodging themselves within the multi-layered windowpane.

Bulletproof. A SIG isn't gonna cut it. I'd need a rifle with armor piercing rounds. Even then the window's polycarbonate layers would take significant abuse before failing.

I inspect the glass closely. How could I break it open?

Whazzat? Something red just flitted past the periphery of my vision. I try to spin around.

A crack of gunfire.

I'm dead before I know what hit me.

The End

As long as I'm here ...

The nearer truck is a plain-Jane white International rig. No trailer. I step onto the passenger-side running board and let myself into the cabin.

A red Little Tree air freshener hangs from the rear-view mirror. No scent. Must be old.

I open the glove box. It has a stack of maps and an open pack of Doublemint gum. Three sticks left. I slide a paper-wrapped stick from the pack. It snaps at the gentlest touch. The loose end, still in the wrapper, dangles from fingers.

Yeah. Definitely old. I toss the gum back into the glove box and pull out the maps. There are dozens of them, at least one for every state. The driver was a real long-hauler.

One question answered: Looks like I'm in the good old U.S. of A.

Maps of New England are towards the top of the stack. A good sign I'm close to home. I can smell the chowder now.

Nothing else to see here. On to the next truck, a blue Mack, also without a payload.

I try the driver-side door. Locked.

The passenger side is more welcoming. The door swings open.

Yech. A pungent odor overwhelms my nose.

Death.

A corpse is slumped against the driver-side door, rotting away. Caucasian male, six foot or so, dressed in hospital-blue scrubs. Maybe a doctor? I slide up into the passenger seat for a closer look.

I'm no coroner. But judging from the level of decay this guy is at least six months gone. Possibly more. The air here is dry. Decomposition would occur slowly.

On the floor mat, near the man's feet, is a SIG Sauer semi-automatic pistol. Must've been a suicide.

I'm glad he locked the driver-side door. If he hadn't I would've been knocked over by his corpse. Unfortunately, his conscientiousness doesn't tell me why he chose to suck down a bullet.

But something else might: A bright yellow sheet of paper, taped above the stereo controls.

A note. I peel it from the console.

Read the note.
Turn to Section 62.

I have a confession to make.

I haven't been on-board with all of your decisions. Yet despite my disagreements, I've kept my mouth shut and dutifully followed your every command.

That obedience ends now.

Rage. Yeti rage!

I lock eyes with my reflection. Horrific. Hideous.

Slam my fist into the mirror.

Impact unexpectedly powerful.

Glass shards fly. Shred my gown. Pierce my skin.

The storm ceases. Glass crashes to the floor.

Silence.

That's when I realize I can't breathe.

I reach for my throat. A jagged chunk of glass is lodged in it.

I pull it out.

Severed windpipe. Minutes to live.

I fall to my knees. Choke on my own blood.

You should've let me trim my beard.

This is your fault. Thanks a lot.

The End

98

Before I can pull away, the machine spits out two steel crescents. The crescents snap together to form a cuff over my wrist, binding my hand to the scanner.

Looks like I'll be here for a while.

A strange energy passes through me. My hair and beard stand on end.

Oh God. I know what's coming. I close my eyes. Brace for it.

The electricity hits me like a Humvee. My nerves are on fire.

I keep my lips zipped — no screaming. I'll face my fate with dignity.

I drop to one knee. A whiff of burning flesh wafts into my nose.

It's two minutes to midnight for me.

Maybe not even two.

The End

A table full of goodies. Let's see what there is to play with.

I sift through the haphazard stacks of gear. I turn up a few assault rifles, a couple of Desert Eagles, a handful of frag grenades, and two bulletproof Kevlar vests, among other things.

As I'm digging, something catches on my pinky finger.

I extract my hand from the clutter. A small, dark metal ring is wrapped around my pinky. A narrow spike protrudes from it.

Grenade pin.

Oh crap.

Run! Go, John, go! Johnny be good!

I only make it a few feet before the Pompeii-in-a-pineapple erupts. A torrential wave of heat crashes into my back. Knocks me forward. Slams me to the floor.

Double vision. Can't focus. Ringing ears.

The smell of burning flesh. My flesh?

I lie on my chest, unable to move. I hang in there a few more minutes before passing out.

I was so close to the exit. Too bad close only counts in horseshoes and … never mind.

The End

100

I'm hovering. Floating amid a syrupy black haze.

Wisps of smoke swirl around me. Like gray tufts of cotton candy.

Where am I? How did I get here?

My short-term memory is as foggy as my surroundings.

I was in Egypt. I lost my arm there. And then ... I woke up in an abandoned hospital?

Was the hospital a dream? Or is this the dream?

A voice bellows through the dark mist: "Hello, Mr. Osborne."

I spin around.

No one here.

"Who said that?" I ask.

The unseen presence clears his disembodied throat. "There's no need to trouble yourself with such trifles, Mr. Osborne. Just listen."

I cross my arms. I'm listening.

Continue to next page.

"You and your reader friend have uncovered the secret of Room 100. You may claim your prize at the following web address."

"The hell are you talking about?"

"Please … Please …" The man's voice cracks, revealing a nasally timbre. He coughs to clear his throat. Collects himself. "Please wait a moment. The answer will appear in neon before you."

I furrow my brow. Something about this voice is familiar. Have I chatted with this guy before? A figure in jeans and a black t-shirt materializes in my mind's eye.

A bright orange line of text coalesces among the wisps of black:

http://simplyunbound.com/room-100/

"Instructions for claiming your prize lie here, Mr. Osborne and reader friend," the voice says.

"Who is this reader friend you keep babbling about?" I ask.

"Please don't muddle your mind with such minutiae, Mr. Osborne. Now, I ask that you manually return to the place from where you came. Or if you'd prefer, I can send you back to the beginning of the adventure."

Uh … right?

Unlose myself. Go back to the beginning.
Turn to Section 1.

101

I want out. Exit door it is.

The door's two panels meet at a seam. A vertical line.

I choose a point near the line. Pull back my arm. Throw a whopper of a punch.

My fist leaves an impression. Slightly shallower than the ones I made in the previous door.

Must be thicker steel. Not thick enough.

I punch.

Slam.

Clobber.

Smash.

My arm doesn't tire. Zero fatigue. What kind of batteries does it run on?

The steel continues to crumple. A gap appears between the door panels. On the other side is green.

Pure, natural, resplendent green.

Within thirty seconds I've pounded open a hole wide enough to wiggle through. I remove my pistol and grenades. Toss them outside. Squeeze myself through the gap.

My head pokes through first. Before me is an old road, overgrown with grasses and weeds, surrounded by lush forest.

New England?

I pull the rest of my body through. Brace my palms on the dirt road. Extract my legs from the hole. Collapse to the ground.

I did it. I escaped.

I bask in warm sunlight. Don't know where I am. Don't know what season it is. I could be a stone's throw from the Atlantic seaboard. This could be a summer day.

Friends and family could be waiting for me just down this road.

Unlikely? Sure. But I've earned a moment to daydream.

The truth will come soon enough.

The End

102

I eye the door that leads deeper into the corridor. Can my fist make its steel panels beg for mercy? We're about to find out.

I step up to the door and swing. My fist crashes into the steel door. I feel slight discomfort in my knuckles, my nerves informing me that yes, I am punching pure steel.

Discomfort. Not pain.

The result: An inch-deep crater in the metal.

I pound again and again. My confidence grows. The divots become deeper and deeper. Though I don't know how, my left arm is getting the job done. The pock-marked door won't hold up for long.

As I punch and punch, that familiar robotic voice speaks:

"Please remain calm and wait for the appropriate personnel to come to your assistance. Do not try to escape, or I will have no choice but to respond with lethal force."

Message ignored. My arm flies forward. Between the clangs of knuckles against steel, I perceive a subtle hissing sound.

My eyes dart up. The air overhead shimmers. Like the haze of heat above the deserts in Egypt.

It's cool here. I'm guessing the haze isn't from heat, but from gas. Invisible gas must be permeating the room.

Is the gas narcotic? Lethal? I'd rather not find out.

I slam the door. Faster. Harder. My arm perforates the steel like a secretary's hole punch. The cavity's jagged edge tears at my sleeve as I extract my limb from the hole.

I throw another punch. Pound the area around the hole. Widen the gap.

Brain feels foggy. Like the gas is seeping into my skull. Settling over my thoughts.

Still, my left arm doesn't relent. Soon I've made a hole just wide enough to slither through.

I hammer down the sharp edges. Climb in headfirst. Thrust myself through to the other side. Belly flop onto the floor like a seal.

I expect a bruise or two when I wake up tomorrow. The belly flop will leave a mark.

With a grunt, I force myself to my feet and look ahead.

You have gotta be kidding me. An identical steel door blocks my path. I'm in another short stretch of corridor. Another five-meter-long prison.

In total, this corridor extends for thousands of meters. Maybe over a mile. If every door I break through leads to another ...

I hear gas whisper overhead. No time to stop. I must keep going.

I bash the next door. The steel gives way, quickly accumulating a collection of fist-sized indentations. My arm doesn't seem to tire. I could throw megaton punches all day.

But then why do I feel so sleepy?

The gas is making me drowsy. I must escape the gas. Punch harder. Faster.

A few lungfuls of toxic gas won't stop John Osborne.

Not for long, they won't. But maybe for just a few minutes they will. I bet if I take a short nap I'll wake up feeling great.

My punching slows. Weakens.

I relent. Sit on the floor. Lean against the door. Close my eyes.

Just a short nap and everything will be fine.

Everything will be absolutely ... perfectly ... splendidly ... fine ...

The End

A vehicular escape, Hollywood-style? Sounds fun.

I peer into one of the FMTV's canvas-covered beds. There's space for over a dozen soldiers and their gear. Empty space.

I hop into the cabin. Check the ignition. Instead of an ignition switch I find a thumb reader. I try my thumb. The scanner doesn't acknowledge my touch.

Technology. Forever making life difficult. I exit the cabin and move on.

The second FMTV uses a starter switch. Exactly what I was looking for. I give it a flick.

Nothing. Deader than my great uncle Osborne.

I try the last truck. Also a switch-starter. Its engine refuses to turn over, too.

Dead batteries? Electrical problems? Could be anything.

I jump out of the cabin.

Three trucks and no luck. I could go back and attempt to hot-wire the first FMTV, though I'm guessing it's just as dead as the other two. The alternative is to have a closer look at the exit door.

Try to hack the first truck's the thumb reader.
Turn to Section 108.

Go back to the exit door.
Turn to Section 85.

104

I aim the SIG at a crate and unload a round. The bullet impacts the wood with a harsh crunch. Leaves a small hole.

A few more rounds and the hole will be big enough for me to get a solid grip on it. Then I can pry it open.

I pull the trigger indiscriminately.

One shot.

Two.

Th —

Light bursts from the crate. A supersonic boom punctures my eardrums. Heat scorches my face. Explosive force hurls me into the air.

Wooden splinters — thousands of them — penetrate my skin. Slashing, clawing, burrowing.

My spine crashes to the floor.

Too much pain. Muscles won't respond.

I broke a cardinal rule of gun safety: Always know your target and what's beyond it.

I close my eyes. It hurts to breathe. I pray the pain won't last long.

The End

105

I reach behind me. My hand scours the table for a gun.

My eyes leave the man for a fraction of a second.

I glimpse the table's wares. Snatch a M27. Thrust its stock against my shoulder.

When I look up the man is gone.

I cautiously circle the nearby tables.

Where did he go? Was he ever here at all? Am I hallucinating? Maybe the doctors here didn't stop with my arm. Maybe they also operated on my brain.

In any case, I won't let my guard down again.

Reassess the situation.
Turn to Section 119.

I'm alone. Trapped in a mysterious facility. And I don't know why.

I step up to the door and slam both fists against it. The dull thump of vented frustration rumbles through the air.

I pull my arms back. There's a divot where my left fist hit the door.

Was it there before? I don't think so ... I cock an eyebrow at my left arm. Twist the limb back and forth. Examine it.

The black hairs glisten. The arm looks natural. Real. Ordinary. But ...

I curl my hand into a fist and close my eyes. My fingers won't be happy if I'm wrong about this. I take a deep breath. Summon my strength. Launch my fist at the door.

My punch connects. The steel buckles from the force. My knuckles dig into the door.

I retract my arm. The crater in the door is two inches deep. My hand, meanwhile, feels good as new.

I don't know what this arm is. But it sure ain't the limb I was born with.

I wind up. Bludgeon the door. Again. And again. And again. Soon the left panel is pock-marked with fist-sized craters.

My next blow breaks through the steel. The hole consumes my arm up to my shoulder. I wrest the limb from the hole.

Outside I see grass. Lush plant life. Staid old trees. An overgrown road.

Only a volley of jabs separates me from freedom. My fist attacks the door with renewed eagerness. No matter how many punches I throw, the arm doesn't tire. My barrage continues until the hole is almost big enough to squeeze through.

I tear at the hole's jagged rim. Rip the gap wider. Hammer to blunt the sharp edges. I have a carpenter's toolbox in an arm-sized package.

When the gap is wide enough to wriggle through, I remove the Desert Eagle and the grenades from my belt and toss them outside.

I glance back over my shoulder and say, "*annyeong.*"

Struggling through the hole is like packing the last sardine into the can. A tight squeeze. I brace my palms on the road outside. Shimmy through like a seal. Flop to the weed-ridden ground.

I'm free. Out.

Out where?

I'm no forest ranger. But it looks like I'm in a temperate area, surrounded by a mixture of evergreens and deciduous trees.

Comfortable temperature. Probably late spring or early summer. Could be Europe, North America, or even Russia.

Maybe I'm back home on the East Coast.

I collect the grenades and pistol. Rise to my feet. Brush the dirt off my fatigues.

Behind me is the battered steel door, set in a rocky hillside. The only clue that there's a facility within. Printed in white across the two dark chrome panels are the letters

MH-ZERO

If I were a passerby I'd assume it was an abandoned mine. Mine Hole Zero.

I know better. But I don't know as much as I'd

like.

What is MH-ZERO? A U.S. Marines hospital? A military hospital? The door provides no further insight.

Time to hit the road. The overgrown dirt path, my conduit back into the world, veers into the forest.

I have a vague inkling that the world I'm returning to isn't the one I left.

The End

Right. I shouldn't shoot the crate. That would be a violation of basic firearm safety.

I venture back the way I came. Through the hallway. Towards the room I initially escaped. My fortunes seem gloomier than they did when I first woke up. A terrible virus, and God knows what else, waits for me outside.

I step past the room I woke up in. Glance at the restraining table I was strapped to. How many years did I lie there?

The hallway ahead is long. Rooms line both sides. Through the windows I see they look much like the room I woke up in.

Operating tables. Monitor arrays. Trinkets scattered about.

No people.

Wait. I see a corpse rotting in a corner, face half gone. I stand corrected. There are people. Dead people.

My interest is piqued. I step into room. Its layout is familiar.

I kneel beside the decaying body. Set my SIG on the floor.

The remains are far gone. Covered by ratty medical scrubs. How long has this person been rotting here? How did they die?

A whooshing sound. A sharp thud.

I glance back. The door has closed.

Goddamnit.

A monotone voice broadcasts overhead: "Unauthorized weaponry detected in Room 126. Initiating security measures. Please remain calm."

The SIG. The pistol plunged me into this mess. Maybe it can help me scrape my way back out. You decide.

Try to gun my way out of the room.
Turn to Section 95.

Be a good boy. Don't touch the SIG.
Wait to see what happens.
Turn to Section 73.

I return to the first truck. Before taking drastic measures, I try the thumb reader one last time. *Nada.*

I tear off the panel below the steering column. The starter is connected to a smorgasbord of electronics.

Wires. Capacitors. Diodes. Computer chips.

This ain't your grandpa's hot-wire job.

I separate the bundles of wires. Try touching their tips together in various combinations. Hope for a spark.

It's no use. Likely a dead battery.

Three trucks and not a working one among them.

Nothing works. Nothing!

Hammersnap!

I flick switches on the console at random. Right side. Left side. Throw 'em up. Push 'em down.

A metal toggle switch snaps free. Slips from of my fingers. Flies towards my face.

The metal stem pierces my eye like a bullet. Shoots through my brain. Lodges itself in the back of my skull.

Some men don't know their own strength.

Count me among them.

The End

"You say you're a writer. What do you plan to write next? Will you write more adventures about me, or are you conceiving other things?"

Henry purses his lips. "Must you continue cracking jokes about me conceiving things? I didn't even use the word!"

"Actually, you did. Because if you are who you say you are, anything I say is something you wrote."

Henry grumbles and massages his temples. "How about you let me answer your question? Or rather, the question that I asked myself through you, if you'd prefer to think of it that way."

I'd prefer to get out of here. That option doesn't seem to be on the table.

Henry continues: "The next story is a mystery even to me. There are a few *Northland Adventures* germinating in my story garden. *The Northland Chronicles 4* also needs my attention. Beyond that, I have a few sci-fi thriller ideas bouncing around my head, with the tentative names *Wavelength, World Apart,* and *MindBind.* Finally, I have a story in mind that involves a stream of life known as The Vir. But alas, I'm getting ahead of myself. So many stories, so little time!"

"The Vir?"

"Indeed." Henry frowns. He says nothing more.

Think of what to say next.
Turn to Section 77.

My fingers tremble.

Never have I so willingly thrown myself into such a cesspool of uncertainty.

It's

DISCO TIME

Two panels slide open, one on either side of the monitor array, revealing a stereo speaker system.

Electric motors whir. Three balls lower from the ceiling. They're decorated with mirrors and colored lights.

Music plays. Drums. Guitar. Keyboard. A pleasant framework. Horns, strings, and bass join the mix. A singer yelps. Colors dance across the walls, flashing and flickering in time with the music.

My fingers snap to the beat. They refuse to stop. The music seeps into my body. Penetrates my heart. My hips shake with the passion of the night. My feet shuffle like tomorrow will never come.

The singer shouts out, insisting that everybody have fun tonight.

Have fun.

Wang chung.

Have fun.

Wang chung.

I look at the computer screen.

Can't stop dancing.

A ginormous button on display reads:

NEXT SONG

The party must go on.

Throw on the next tune.
Turn to Section 45.

111

Relax, John. You got this.

I press my palm to the scanner.

Strange ... My body hair rises. Stands on end. Almost as though lightning is about to —

A metal cuff pops up from the scanning panel's lower edge and shackles my wrist.

A thick cuff. No breaking free.

A titanic wave of electricity courses through my body.

Pain wracks my every cell. Is that burning flesh I smell?

The electricity doesn't relent. The last thing I feel is my bowels expelling their contents into my pants.

The End

I stare down the long corridor to the right. What's down there?

May as well start walking.

The steel walls are spartan, decorated only by glass windows. Through the windows and open doorways are rooms, identical to the room I woke up in. Each has an operating table and an array of computer monitors.

Were all of these rooms occupied at one point? Were all the patients military men like me?

The rooms are numbered. Right now I'm in the low hundreds. As I pass room 126, I see person resting in the corner. I rush in to check it out.

The person is wearing hospital scrubs.

The person is ... dead.

So much for asking her what the hell is going on.

Continue to next page.

I take a knee beside the corpse. Looks like she died years ago. Her scrubs are more holes than fabric.

Not sure how she died. I don't see a weapon.

Encouraging: People used to work here. Discouraging: No one has cleaned up this pile of bones.

Am I the only living soul in this place?

As I stand up, I feel a tingling in my bladder. How long has it been since my last trip to the restroom? I should probably relieve myself soon.

Whip out Little John and take care of business in the corner of the room.
Turn to Section 60.

Find a proper place to relieve myself.
Turn to Section 115.

Be prepared. That's the Scout Motto.

I return to the row of lockers. I didn't check all of them. I quickly find another one with its door ajar.

The main compartment is empty. I reach up to the top shelf. There's something thin and leathery up here. Almost like a rope.

A rope that moves? A chill runs down my spine.

A long, scaly body slides across the gap between the locker and the open door.

A snake. The body of a snake.

Where is its head? It could be behind me, preparing to plunge its fangs into my neck.

I turn slowly. Very, very slowly. Are snakes stimulated by movement? Colors? Smells?

I find the snake behind me. We lock eyes with one another. It sticks out its little red tongue and hisses at me.

The tongue waggles back and forth. Back and forth.

Suddenly the snake's jaws snap open. It lunges at my throat. Digs its fangs into my windpipe.

Arrrrrrhhh!

I stumble back into the locker. The snake retreats, scaling down the door and slipping away across the ground.

I try to breathe. My breaths are shallow and raspy. Hollow imitations of the real deal.

I try to stand, only to stagger forward. No air to my lungs. No air to my brain.

I fall to my knees. Hit the locker door on the way down. Collapse to the floor.

I hear the snake slithering across the floor,

drawing close. He must see me lying here. Must sense that I'm helpless.

The snake's rough, leathery skin creeps across my neck. Wraps around my throat.

I can't breathe.

I imagine my face turning blue. Red. Purple. Imagine my eyes popping out of their sockets.

Why didn't I grab the snake and crush it in my left hand? It's a good idea, but it's too late. Too late to spare me from

The End

114

The lockers, steel-framed and painted green, look straight out of middle school. Each has a latch for a padlock. Many are locked with black-faced combination locks. Others employ keys or other protection mechanisms.

Going down the row of lockers, I find one that's unlocked. Inside is a compartment suitable for hanging clothes. Atop the main compartment is a small shelf.

The locker is bare. I move on.

The next one I check offers better returns. I find a set of light green military fatigues, about my size.

I slip out of my thin hospital gown. Step into the lower half of the fatigues. The waist is a bit loose — previous owner must've had a thing for donuts — but it'll suffice.

Shirt is next. I guide my arms through the sleeves.

Odd ... a pink band encircles my left shoulder. The band, a lumpy ring of scar tissue, looks like it was branded into my skin. It sits on the line where my torso ends and my arm begins.

I rotate my, testing the joint. Full range of motion. No pain or weakness. The entire limb seems to be in working order.

What happened to my arm? If only there was someone here I could ask.

I pull the green shirt over my shoulders. I need to focus on escaping. Questions can come later.

On the locker's top shelf I find black socks, a pair of all-terrain boots, and a pistol holster. The boots are a little tight, but the price is right.

Baggy clothes, tight shoes. Like I said: Too many Krispy Kremes.

I strap the holster around my thigh. There's a table full of guns behind me. I can choose a piece from it.

I toss the hospital gown in the locker and slam the door shut. What's next?

Check more lockers.
Turn to Section 69.

Select a gun for my holster.
Turn to Section 87.

I don't care if this place is emptier than a Mormon tabernacle in Tibet. Certain taboos deserve respect. I won't forfeit my humanity.

I step back into the hallway and hunt for a restroom. Ahead, I spot a pair of doors, one for each gender.

Little boys' room, please.

Inside the door I find an ordinary restroom. Three closed stalls, for taking care of serious business, abut one wall. A row of urinals lines the other. Two sinks round out the facilities. Above the sinks hangs a mirror.

I approach a white porcelain urinal. Lift my gown. Let it flow. Never has relieving myself felt so ... relieving. For all I know it's been years since I last took a proper piss. When I'm done, I lower my hospital gown and press the lever. Clear water rushes to sweep away all traces of my dirty business.

Dirty business, indeed. I'd better wash my hands. I step over to the sink.

Continue to next page.

Holy Philly cheesesteak! I recoil at the sight of myself in the mirror.

More hair than a lion's mane. A beard mangy enough to conceal a small child.

I'd seen vague reflections of myself in the windows. I didn't imagine I looked like this. This is a problem I need to fix soon. Soon as in now.

Lo and behold: A pair of scissors rest beside the sink. Looks like they're ready to snip.

Apparently there is a God.

Chop off my hair and beard.
Turn to Section 51.

Deal with it later.
Turn to Section 19.

I hop into the nearest truck and check the ignition.

No starter switch. Only a thumb reader.

Right. The military was phasing out switch-based ignitions for ones that require ID. These new ones are tricky to jump start. I'd be willing to try, but let's check the other trucks first.

I climb into the next truck's cabin. Here we go: A good, old-fashioned ignition switch. Must be an older model.

I crank it. No sound. Nothing. The engine doesn't even humor me.

Dead battery, or a more serious problem? Maybe I should try another approach.

Recklessly unload a few rounds from the M27 rifle in frustration.
Turn to Section 82.

Keep cool. Leave the truck. Go to the door. Bash my way to freedom.
Turn to Section 79.

117

Trying to blow the door open could be dangerous. Pounding on it sounds like a waste of time. Venturing back into the facility and searching for another exit looks like the best choice among bad options.

I did leave at least one path unexplored. The left branch of the long hallway. Something useful could be hiding down that way.

I cross the sunlit room, back toward the long, narrow corridor.

My feet grow heavier with each step. My instincts scream that this is stupid. That I shouldn't be leaving this place, so close to the exit. But my mind is made up. No reason to second-guess myself now.

I pass into the corridor. Not half a dozen steps in, I hear a heavy thud.

I whip my head around. A door has fallen closed behind me. Printed across it are the words

MAIN EXIT

I curse under my breath. So I was on the right track.

Another thud resounds through the corridor. The crash of a second door dropping closed behind me.

This just keeps getting better and better. I'm cut off in both directions. Why the hell did I come back this way?

I slam my fists against the main exit door. The impact is unexpectedly loud. Resonant. Deafening.

Where my left hand hit the door, I find a fist-shaped indentation.

The hell? Did my hand just leave an impression in solid steel?

Hmm ...

Maybe the arm has been imbued with extra strength. An operation would explain the peculiar ring of scar tissue around my shoulder, as well as the arm's indifference to electricity and extreme heat.

From speakers overhead, that dull female voice drones:

"Please remain calm and wait for the appropriate personnel to come to your assistance."

Color me amused. No one is coming to my assistance. I have to bust out of here on my own.

This arm may be the key.

Pound the main exit door.
Turn to Section 90.

Beat on the door that leads deeper into the facility.
Turn to Section 102.

118

Only one thing matters: Getting out of here. Every other concern is on hold.

I snoop around the computer's hard drive. It's loaded with documents and system files.

Thousands of files. Millions. More than I have time to browse through.

Search. I need to use the search function.

Here we go. A blinking cursor beckons me to enter my request.

Floor plans

I hit enter. No results.

Let's try again:

Escape

Enter.

One result. A video.

Captain Jack and the Great Orifice Escape

Not kosher. I'll steer clear.

I try to rub my chin, only to discover I have a monstrous mass of facial hair hanging from it. A beard? I'll have to deal with it soon. Very soon. But not now.

What to type next?

Security

Three results.

Sadistic Security Services, LLC

Security Control Panel

Security in a Large Package

This computer's operator was a strange, strange man.

I open the security control panel. It's packed with security options. Cameras. Lights. Door locks.

Looks like I can control everything.

Surprisingly, there's no password protection. What option should I play with first?

Try to disable the security systems.
Turn to Section 65.

Find a way to open the door.
Turn to Section 72.

Adjust the lighting.
Turn to Section 49.

119

I want only one thing:

I want out of here.

I stalk through the room. Before long I find a two-paneled metal door.

EXIT

It's big enough to drive a truck through. Beside it is a hand scanner.

My hand print didn't work before. I doubt it'll work now.

I see a couple of other ways to huff and puff and blow the door down.

Bash the door with my arm until it gives.
Turn to Section 79.

Start up an FMTV and drive it into the door.
Turn to Section 116.

120

Time to explore. I hop to my feet. The room has a high ceiling. Light dithers in from translucent skylights.

Sunlight. Freedom.

Three military trucks — six-wheeled FMTVs with green canvas covers over their beds, suitable for carrying either troops or supplies — are parked here. All three vehicles face different directions, like they were parked in a hurry.

Near the trucks are tables haphazardly stacked with military gear. Behind the tables, metal closets line the room's walls.

Continue to next page.

I approach a table. I'm familiar with most of this gear. Standard issue assault rifles. Desert Eagle semi-automatics. Pineapple grenades. Kevlar vests.

I take one of the assault rifles, a high-powered M27.

Stock against my shoulder. Eye to the sights. Finger around the trigger.

Feels good.

"Hello there, John."

I freeze. The voice came from behind.

How did someone sneak up on me? Why didn't I hear footsteps?

The voice sounded friendly. Suspiciously friendly.

I'm not in a trusting mood. But I'll trust you. What should I do?

Set down the gun, raise both hands high,
and turn to face the mysterious man.
Turn to Section 94.

Twirl around and take aim.
Turn to Section 86.

121

I hammer the keys.

✳✳
✳✳✳✳✳✳✳✳✳✳✳

That should do it.

Enter!

The asterisks disappear. A giant yellow smiley face pops up on screen.

"Nice Try!"

The monitor goes black. A cell-phone-sized slat opens beside the keyboard. A small, worm-like object emerges from the hole. A camera lens is mounted onto its tiny face.

The camera hovers up and down, examining me. I give it a dirty look.

The worm quickly pulls back into its hole. Coward.

A red light materializes from above the monitor, tracing a thin line through the dust particles in the air.

A laser?

The beam pinpoints the bridge of my nose.

Oh shit.

Flash. Bang.

The End

122

The next song starts without delay. It's familiar. I might've heard it in a roller skating rink.

It opens with trumpet:

Da, da da, da da dada dada da.

Da, da da, da da dada dada da.

Da, dadada, dadada.

Young man! Down on your luck? No place to go?

Six colorfully clad figures appear in my mind's eye.

A police officer. A GI. A biker in black leather. A construction worker. A cowboy. A Native America chieftain.

Never has my future been so bright. My arms fly into the air.

Whyyyyy, em see ay!

Whyyyyy, em see ay!

With a mighty leap, I bound up onto the restraining table. Once shackled, I'm now free. What was a prison is now a dance hall.

I pose for the cameras. Music pumps through these veins. I'm a star.

My eyes turn to the computer screen.

next song?

I backflip off the table. Spin to face the computer console.

Let's see what's next.

Find out what familiar sounds await me.
Turn to Section 45.

I type 4f5gDser7 and press enter.

The password prompt disappears. Must've gotten it right.

The security options are extensive. I can disable cameras, shut down defensive mechanisms, activate or deactivate covert security measures, and override password protection on all network computers.

So many choices. Where to start?

Strange. A tiny camera has emerged from the console. It's looking at me. Observing.

Let's get rid of it. I select:

Disable Cameras

Nothing happens. I click again.

Again.

Nothing. Maybe the controls are laggy?

I return to browsing the security panel. The camera retreats. Whatever I did must've worked.

That's what I assume until I notice the red beam targeting my forehead.

An explosion of light.

A deafening blast.

I'm dead before I can fall out of my chair.

The End

Henry J. Olsen was once a quiet kid in a small Wisconsin town. Now he travels the world and writes tales of adventure. He presently lives in Kaohsiung, Taiwan.

Catch up with him at http://simplyunbound.com.

Also By Henry J. Olsen

♫ *Shake shake shake*
Shake shake shake ♫